The Pharisee And The Publican

John Bunyan

Contents

THE PHARISEE AND THE PUBLICAN

BY

John Bunyan

THE PHARISEE AND THE PUBLICAN.
by John Bunyan

Two men went up into the temple to pray; the one a Pharisee, and the other a Publican. The Pharisee stood and prayed thus with himself; God, I thank thee, that I am not as other men are, extortioners, unjust, adulterers, or even as this Publican. I fast twice in the week, I give tithes of all that I possess. And the Publican, standing afar off would not lift up so much as his eyes unto heaven, but smote upon his breast, saying, God be merciful to me a sinner.-- Luke, xviii. 10-13.

In the beginning of this chapter you read of the reason of the parable of the unjust judge and the poor widow; namely, to encourage men to pray. "He spake a parable to this end, that men ought always to pray, and not to faint;" and a most sweet parable for that purpose it is: for if through importunity, a poor widow woman may prevail with an unjust judge, and so consequently with an unmerciful and hardhearted tyrant, how much more shall the poor, afflicted, distressed, and tempted people of God, prevail with, and obtain mercy at the hands of, a loving, just, and merciful God? The unjust judge would not hearken to, nor regard the cry of, the poor widow, for a while: "But afterward he said within himself, Though I fear not God, nor regard man; yet because this widow troubleth me, I will avenge her, lest by her continual coming she weary me." "Hark," saith Christ, "what the unjust judge saith." "And shall not God avenge his own elect, which cry day and night unto him?--I tell you that he will avenge them speedily."

This is therefore a very comfortable parable to such of the saints as are under hard usage by reason of evil men, their might and tyranny: for by it we are taught to believe and expect, that God, though for a while he seemeth not to regard, yet will, in due time and season, arise and set such in safety from them that puff at them;

Psalm xii. 4.

Let the good Christian pray always; let him pray, and not faint at seeming delays; for if the widow by importunity prevailed with the unjust judge, how much more shall he with his heavenly Father. "I tell you," says Christ, "that he will avenge them speedily."

But now, forasmuch as this parable reacheth not (so directly) the poor Publican in the text, therefore our Lord begins again, and adds to that other parable, this parable which I have chosen for my text; by which he designeth two things: First, The conviction of the proud and self-conceited Pharisee: Secondly, The raising up and healing of the cast down and dejected Publican. And observe it, as by the first parable he chiefly designeth the relief of those that are under the hands of cruel tyrants, so by this he designeth the relief of those that lie under the load and burden of a guilty and disquieted conscience.

This therefore is a parable that is full of singular comfort to such of the sinners in the world that are clogged with guilt and sense of sin; and that lie under the apprehensions of, and that are driven to God by the sense of the judgment that for sin is due unto them.

In my handling of this text, I shall have respect to these things -

1. To the persons in the text.
2. To the condition of the persons in the text.
3. To the conclusion that Christ makes upon them both.

First, For the persons. They were, as you see, far one from another in their own apprehension of themselves; one good, the other bad; but yet in the judgment of the law, both alike, both the same, both sinners; for they both stood in need of mercy. True, the first mentioned did not see it, as the other poor sinner did; but that altereth not the case: he that is in the judgment of the law a sinner, is in the judgment of the law for sin condemned, though in his own judgment he be ever so righteous.

Men must not be judged, or justified, according to what themselves do think, but according to the verdict and sentence that cometh out of the mouth of God about them. Now, the sentence of God is, "All have sinned:" "There is none righteous, no, not one;" Rom. iii. It is no matter, then, what the Pharisee did think of himself; God by his word hath proclaimed him a sinner: a sinner, by reason of original sin; a sinner, by reason of actual transgression. Personally, therefore, with reference to the true nature of their state, they both were sinners, and both by the law under condemnation. True, the Publican's leprosy was outward; but the Pharisee's leprosy was inward: his heart, his soul, his spirit, was as foul, and had as much the plague of sin, as had the other in his life or conversation.

Secondly, As to their conditions (I do not mean by condition, so much a habit of mind, as the state that they had each of them put themselves into by that mind.) "The one," says the text, "was a Pharisee, the other a Publican." A Pharisee: that is, one that hath chosen to himself such a course of life. A Publican: that is, one that hath chosen to himself such a course of life. These terms, therefore, shew the divers courses of life that they had put themselves into. The Pharisee, as he thought, had put himself into a condition for heaven and glory; but the Publican was for this world and his lusts. Wherefore when the Pharisee stands in the temple, he boasteth of himself and good condition, but condemneth the Publican, and bitterly inveigheth against him. But, as I said, their personal state, by the law, was not at all changed. The Pharisee made himself never the better; the Publican also abode in his place.

Indeed the Publican is here found to recant, and repent of his condition, and of the condition that he had put himself into; and the Pharisee to boast of his. But the Publican's repentance was not of himself, but of God, who can also, yea, and sometimes it is evident (Acts ix.) he doth, make Pharisees also repent of that condition that they have chosen to be in themselves; Phil. iii. 3-8. The Pharisee, therefore, in commending of himself, makes himself never the better; the Publican also, in condemning of himself, makes himself never the worse. Nay, contrariwise, the Pharisee, by commending of himself, makes himself much the worse, ver. 14; and the Publican, by condemning of himself, makes himself much the better. "I tell you (says Christ) this man went down to his house justified rather than the other; for every one that exalteth himself shall be abased: and he that humbleth himself shall be exalted."

But, I say, as to men's commending of themselves, yea, though others should commend them also, that availeth, to God-ward, nothing at all. "For not he that commendeth himself is approved, but whom the Lord commendeth." So then, men in "measuring themselves by themselves, and comparing themselves among themselves, are not wise;" 2 Cor. x. 12.

Now, this was the way of the Pharisee; I am not, saith he, as other men: I am no extortioner, nor unjust, no adulterer, nor yet as this Publican.

"Two men went up into the temple to pray;" and they two, as I said, as opposite one to the other, as any two men that ever went thither to pray. One of them was over righteous, and the other wicked over much. Some would have thought, had they not by the word of Christ been otherwise described, that they had been both of the same religion; for they both went up into the temple to pray; yea, both to pray, and that at the same time, as if they did it by appointment, by agreement; but there was no such thing. The one was a Pharisee, the other a Publican: for so saith the after words: and therefore persons as opposite as light and darkness, as fire and water; I mean, as to their apprehensions one of another. The Pharisee could not abide the Publican, nor could the Publican brook the Pharisee; and yet both went up into the temple to pray. It is strange to see, and yet it is seen, that men cross in their minds, cross in their principles, cross in their apprehensions; yea, and cross in their prayers too, should yet meet together in the temple to pray.

"Two men;" men not of the middle sort, and them too picked out of the best and worst that was: two men, a Pharisee, and a Publican.

To be a Pharisee was in those days counted honourable for religion, and for holiness of life. A Pharisee was a man of esteem and repute among the Jews, though it is a term of reproach with us; else Paul would not at such a time as he did it, have said, "Men and brethren, I am a Pharisee, the son of a Pharisee;" Acts xxiii, 6; Phil. iii. 5. For now he stood upon his purgation and justification, especially it appears so by the place first named. And far be it from any to think, that Paul would make use of a colour of wickedness, to save thereby himself from the fury of the people.

A Publican was in those days counted one of the vilest of men, as is manifest; because when they are in the word, by way of discrimination, made mention of, they are ranked with the most vile and base; therefore they are joined with sinners--"He eateth with publicans and sinners," and "with harlots." "Publicans and harlots enter into the kingdom of heaven." Yea, when our Lord Christ would have the rebellious professor stigmatized to purpose, he saith, "Let him be to thee as an heathen man and a publican."

We therefore can make no judgment of men upon the outward appearance of them. Who would have thought, but that the Pharisee had been a good man? for he was righteous; for he prayed. And who could have thought, that the other had been a good man? for he was a Publican; a man, by good men and bad men, joined with the worst of men, to wit, with sinners, harlots, heathens.

The Pharisee was a sectarian; the Publican was an officer. The Pharisee, even because he was a sectarian, was had the more in esteem; and the Publican, because he was an officer, was had the more in reproach. To speak a little to both these:

1. The Pharisee was a sectarian; one that deviated, that turned aside in his worshipping from the way of God, both in matter and manner of worship; for such an one I count a sectarian. That he turned aside from the matter, which is the rule of worship, to wit, the written word, it is evident; for Christ saith, that they rejected the commandments of God, and made them of no effect, that they might keep their own traditions. That they turned aside also as to their manner of worship, and became sectarians, there is with no less authority asserted--"For all their works they do for to be seen of men;" Acts xxvi. 5; Mark vii. 9-13; Matt. xxiii. 5.

Now this being none of the order or ordinance of Christ, and yet being chosen by, and stuck to of these sort of men, and also made a singular and necessary part of worship, became a sect, or bottom for those hypocritical factious men to adhere unto, and to make of others disciples to themselves. And that they might be admired, and rendered 'venerable by the simple people to their fellows, they loved to go in long robes; they loved to pray in markets, and in the corners of the streets; they shewed great zeal for the small things of the law, but had only great words for things that were substantial--"They made broad their phylacteries, and enlarged the borders of their garments;" Matt. xxiii.

When I say the Pharisee was a sectarian, I do not mean that every sectarian is a Pharisee. There were the sects of the Herodians, of the Alexandrians, and of the Sadducees, with many others; but to be a Pharisee, was to be of the straitest sect: "After the most straitest sect of our religion, I lived a Pharisee." That, therefore, of all the sects, was the most strait and strict. Therefore, saith he, in another place, "I was taught according to the perfect manner of the law of the fathers." And again, "Touching the law, a Pharisee;" Acts xxii. 3; xxvi. 4-6; Phil. iii. 5. The Pharisee, therefore, did carry the bell, and wear the garland for religion; for he outdid, he went beyond all other sectarians in his day. He was strictest, he was the most zealous; therefore Christ, in his making of this parable, waived all other sects then in being, and pitched upon the Pharisee as the man most meet, by whose rejection he might shew forth and demonstrate the riches of his mercy in its extension to sinners: "Two men went up into the temple to pray; the one a Pharisee:" such a brave man as you have heard.

2. The Publican also went up thither to pray. The Publican, I told you before, was an officer: an officer that served the Romans and himself too; for the Romans at that time were possessors of the land of Jewry (the lot of Israel's inheritance), and the emperor Tiberius Caesar placed over that land four governors, to wit, Pilate, Herod, Philip, and Lysanias; all these were Gentiles, heathens, infidels; and the publicans were a sort of inferior men, to whom was let out to farm, and so men that were employed by these to gather up the taxes and customs that the heathens had laid upon the Jews to be paid to the emperor; Luke ii. 1; iii. 1, 2, 12, 13.

But they were a generation of men that were very injurious in the execution of their office. They would exact and demand more than was due of the people; yea, and if their demands were denied, they would falsely accuse those that so denied them to the governor, and by false accusation obtain the money of the people, and so wickedly enrich themselves, Luke iii. 13, 14; xix. 2, 8. This was therefore grievous to the Jews, who always counted themselves a free people, and could never abide to be in bondage to any. And this was something of the reason, that they were so generally by all the Jews counted so vile and base, and reckoned among the worst of men, even as our informers and bum-bailiffs are with us at this day.

But that which heightened the spirit of the people against them, and that made them so odious and filthy in their eyes, was for that (at least so I think) these publicans were not, as the other officers, aliens, heathens, and Gentiles, but men of their own nation, Jews, and so the brethren of those that they so abused. Had they been Gentiles, it had not been wondered at.

The Publican then was a Jew, a kind of a renegade Jew, that through the love that he had to unjust gains, fell off in his affections from his brethren, adhered to the Romans, and became a kind of servant to them against their brethren, farming the heathenish taxations at the hand of strangers, and exacting of them upon their brethren with much cruelty, falsehood, and extortion. And hence, as I said, it was, that to be a publican, was to be so odious a thing, so vile a sinner, and so grievous a man in the eyes of the Jews. Why, this was the Publican! he was a Jew, and so should have abode with them, and have been content to share with his brethren in their calamities; but contrary to nature, to law, to religion, reason, and honesty, he fell in with the heathen, and took the advantage of their tyranny to poll, to rob, and impoverish his brethren.

But for proof that the Publican was a Jew.

1. Publicans are, even then, when compared with, yet distinguished from, the heathen; "Let him be to thee as an heathen man and a publican," Matt. xviii.; which two terms, I think, must not here be applied to one and the self-same man, as if the heathen was a publican, or the publican a heathen; but to men of two distinct nations, as that publican and harlot is to be understood of sinners of both sexes. The Publican is not an harlot, for he is a man, &c., and such a man as has been described before. So by publicans and sinners, is meant publicans and such sinners as the Gentiles were; or such as, by the text, the Publican is distinguished from: where the Pharisee saith he was not an extortioner, unjust, adulterer, or even as this Publican. Nor can he by "heathen man" intend the person, and by the term publican, the office or place, of the heathen man; but by publican is meant the renegade Jew, in such a place, &c., as is yet further manifested by that which follows. For -

2. Those publicans, even every one of them that by name are made mention of in the New Testament, have such names put upon them; yea, and other circumstances thereunto annexed, as doth demonstrate them to be Jews. I remember the names of no more but three, to wit, Matthew, Levi, and Zaccheus, and they were all Jews.

(1.) Matthew was a Jew, and the same Matthew was a publican; yea, and also afterwards an apostle. He was a Jew, and wrote his gospel in Hebrew: he was an apostle, and is therefore found among the twelve. That he was a publican too, is as evident by his own words; for though Mark and Luke, in their mentioning of his name and apostleship, do forbear to call him a publican (Mark iii. 18; Luke vi. 16); yet when this Matthew comes to speak of himself, he calls himself Matthew the publican (Matth. x. 3); for I count this the self-same Matthew that Mark and Luke make mention of, because I find no other Matthew among the apostles but he: Matthew the publican, Matthew the man so deep in apostacy, Matthew the man of that ill fame among his brethren. Love, in Mark and Luke, when they counted him among the apostles, did cover with silence this his publican state (and it is meet for Peter to call Paul his beloved brother, when Paul himself shall call himself the chief of sinners); but faithfulness to the world, and a desire to be abased, that Christ thereby, and grace by him, might be advanced, made Matthew, in his evangelical writings, call himself by the name of Matthew the publican. Nor has he lost thereby; for Christ again to exalt him (as he hath also done by the apostle Paul), hath set, by his special providence, the testimony that this Matthew hath given of his birth, life, death, doctrine, and miracles, in the front of all the New Testament.

(2.) The next publican that I find by the Testament of Christ, made mention of by name, is Levi, another of the apostles of Jesus Christ. This Levi also, by the Holy Ghost in holy writ, is called by the name of James: not James the brother of John, for Zebedee was his father; but James the son of Alpheus. Now I take this Levi also to be another than Matthew; First, because Matthew is not called the son of Alpheus; and because Matthew and Levi, or James the son of Alpheus, are distinctly counted where the names of the apostles are mentioned (Matt. x. 3) for two distinct persons: and that this Levi, or James the apostle, was a publican, as was the apostle Matthew, whom we mentioned before, is evident; for both Mark and Luke do count him such. First, Mark saith, Christ found him when he called him, as he also found Matthew, sitting at the receipt of custom; yea, Luke words it thus: "He went forth, and saw a publican, named Levi, sitting at the receipt of custom, and he said unto him, Follow me;" Mark ii. 14; Luke v. 27.

Now, that this Levi, or James the son of Alpheus, was a Jew, his name doth well make manifest. Besides, had there been among the apostles any more Gentiles save Simon the Canaanite, or if this Levi James had been here, I think the Holy Ghost would, to distinguish him, have included him in the same discriminating character as he did the other, when he called him "Simon the Canaanite;" Matt. x. 4.

Matthew, therefore, and Levi or James, were both publicans, and, as I think, called both at the same time; were both publican Jews, and made by grace the apostles of Jesus Christ.

(3.) The next publican that I find by name made mention of in the Testament of Christ, is one Zaccheus. And he was a publican; yea, for ought I know, the master of them all. "There was a man," saith Luke, "named Zaccheus, which was the chief among the publicans, and he was rich," Luke xix. 2. This man, Christ saith, was a son of Abraham, that is, as other Jews were; for he spake to stop the mouths of their Pharisaical cavillations. Besides, the Publican shewed himself to be such an one, when under a supposition of wronging any man, he had respect to the Jewish law of restoring four-fold; Exod. xxii. 1; 2 Sam. xii. 6.

It is further manifest that he was a Jew, because Christ puts him among the lost; to wit, among the lost sheep of the house of Israel, ver. 10; and Matt. xv. 24; for Zaccheus was one that might properly be said to be lost, and that in the Jews' account: lost, I say, and that not only in the most common sense, by reason of transgression against the law, but for that he was an apostate Jew, not with reference to heathenish religion, but as to heathenish, cruel, and barbarous actions; and therefore he was, as the other, by his brethren, counted as bad as heathens, Gentiles, and harlots. But salvation is come to this house, saith Christ, and that notwithstanding his publican practice, forasmuch as he also is the son of Abraham.

3. Again, Christ, by the parable of the lost sheep, doth plainly intimate, that the Publican was a Jew. "Then drew near all the publicans and sinners for to hear him, and the Pharisees and Scribes murmured, saying, This man receiveth sinners, and eateth with them."

But by what answer doth Christ repel their objections? Why, he saith, "What man of you having an hundred sheep, if he lose one of them, doth not leave the ninety and nine in the wilderness, and go after that which is lost until he find it?" Doth he not here, by the lost sheep, mean the poor publican? plenty of whom, while he preached this sermon, were there, as objects of the Pharisees' scorn, but of the pity and compassion of Jesus Christ: he did without doubt mean them. For, pray, what was the flock, and who Christ's sheep under the law, but the house and people of Israel? Ezek. xxxiv. 11. So then, who could be the lost sheep of the house of Israel, but such as were Matthew, James, Zaccheus, and their companions in their and such like transgressions?

4. Besides, had not the publicans been of the Jews, how easy had it been for the Pharisees to have objected, that an impertinency was couched in that most excellent parable of the lost sheep? They might have said, We are offended, because thou receivest the publicans, and thou for vindication of thy practice propoundest a parable of lost sheep; but they are the sinners of the house of Israel, and the publicans are aliens and Gentiles. I say, how easily might they thus have objected? but

they knew full well, that the parable was pertinent, for that the publicans were of the Jews, and not of the aliens. Yea, had they not been Jews, it cannot, it must not be thought, that Christ (in sum) should call them so; and yet he did do so, when he called them "lost sheep."

Now, that these publicans were Jews, what follows but that for this they were a great deal the more abominated by their brethren; and (as I have also hinted before) it is no marvel that they were; for a treacherous brother is worse than an open enemy, Psalm lv. 12, 13; for, if to be debauched in an open and common transgression is odious, how odious is it for a brother to be so; for a brother in nature and religion to be so. I say again, all this they did, as both John insinuates, and Zaccheus confesses.

The Pharisee, therefore, was not so good, but the Publican was as bad. Indeed the Publican was a notorious wretch, one that had a way of transgressing by himself; one that could not be sufficiently condemned by the Jews, nor coupled with a viler than himself. It is true, you find him here in the temple at prayer; not because he retained, in his apostacy, conscience of the true religion; but God had awakened him, shewed him his sin, and bestowed upon him the grace of repentance, by which he was not only fetched back to the temple and prayer, but to his God, and to the salvation of his soul.

The Pharisee, then, was a man of another complexion, and good as to his own thoughts of himself; yea, and in the thoughts of others also, upon the highest and better ground by far. The Publican was a notorious sinner: the Pharisee was a reputed righteous man. The Publican was a sinner out of the ordinary way of sinning; and the Pharisee was a man for righteousness in a singular way also. The Publican pursued his villanies, and the Pharisee pursued his righteousness; and yet they both met in the temple to pray: yea, the Pharisee stuck to, and boasted in, the law of God: but the Publican did forsake it, and hardened his heart against his way.

Thus diverse were they in their appearances: the Pharisee very good, the Publican very bad: but as to the law of God, which looked upon them with reference to the state of their spirits, and the nature of their actions, by that they were both found sinners; the Publican an open, outside one, and the Pharisee a filthy, inside one. This is evident, because the best of them was rejected, and the worst of them was received to mercy. Mercy standeth not at the Publican's badness, nor is it enamoured with the Pharisee's goodness: it suffereth not the law to take place on both, though it findeth them both in sin, but graciously embraceth the most unworthy, and leaveth the best to shift for himself. And good reason that both should be dealt with after this manner; to wit, that the word of grace should be justified upon the soul of the penitent, and that the other should stand or fall to that which he had chosen to be his master.

There are three things that follow upon this discourse.

1. That the righteousness of man is not of any esteem with God, as to justification. It is passed by as a thing of naughtiness, a thing not worth the taking notice of. There was not so much as notice taken of the Pharisee's person or prayer, because he came into the temple mantled up in his own good things.

2. That the man that has nothing to commend him to God, but his own good doings, shall never be in favour with him. This also is evident from the text: the Pharisee had his own righteousness, but had nothing else to commend him to God; and therefore could not by that obtain favour with God, but abode still a rejected one, and in a state of condemnation.

3. Wherefore, though we are bound by the law of charity to judge of men according as in appearance they present themselves unto us; yet withal, to wit, though we do so judge, we must leave room for the judgment of God. Mercy may receive him that we have doomed to hell, and justice may take hold on him, whom we have judged to be bound up in the bundle of life. And both these things are apparent by the persons under consideration.

We, like Joseph, are for setting of Manasseh before Ephraim; but God, like Jacob, puts his hands across, and lays his right hand upon the worst man's head, and his left hand upon the best (Gen. xlviii.), to the amazement and wonderment even of the best of men.

"Two men went up into the temple to pray; the one a Pharisee, and the other a Publican. The Pharisee stood and prayed thus with himself; God, I thank thee, that I am not as other men are, extortioners, unjust, adulterers, or even as this Publican. I fast twice in the week I give tithes of all that I possess."

In these words many things are worth the noting. As,

First, The Pharisee's definition of righteousness; the which standeth in two things: 1. In negatives; 2. In positives.

1. In negatives; to wit, what a man that is righteous must not be: "I am no extortioner, no unjust man, no adulterer, nor yet as this Publican."

2. In positives; to wit, what a man that is righteous must be: "I fast twice a-week, I give tithes of all that I possess," &c.

That righteousness standeth in negative and positive holiness is true; but that the Pharisee's definition is, notwithstanding, false, will be manifest by and by. But I will first treat of righteousness in the general, because the text leadeth me to it.

First, then, a man that is righteous, must have negative holiness; that is, he must not live in actual transgressions; he must not be an extortioner, unjust, an adulterer, or as the Publican was. And this the apostle intends, when he saith, "Flee fornication," "Flee youthful lusts," "Flee from idolatry;" and, "Little children keep yourselves from idols;" 1 Cor. vi. 18; x. 14; 2 Tim. ii. 22; 1 John v. 21. For it is a vain thing to talk of righteousness, and that ourselves are righteous, when every observer shall find us in actual transgression. Yea, though a man shall mix his want of negative holiness with some good actions, that will not make him a righteous man. As suppose, a man that is a swearer, a drunkard, an adulterer, or the like, should, notwithstanding this, be open-handed to the poor, be a great executor of justice in his place, be exact in his buying, selling, keeping his promise with his friend, or the like; these things, yea, many more such, cannot make him a righteous man; for the beginning of righteousness is yet wanting in him, which is this negative holiness: for except a man leave off to do evil, he cannot be a righteous man. Negative holiness is therefore of absolute necessity to make one in one's self a righteous man. This therefore condemns them, that count it sufficient if a man have some actions that in themselves, and by virtue of the command, are good, to make him a righteous man, though negative holiness is wanting. This is as saying to the wicked, Thou art righteous, and a perverting of the right way of the Lord: negative holiness, therefore, must be in a man before he can be accounted righteous.

2. As negative holiness is required to declare one a righteous man; so also positive holiness must be joined therewith, or the man is unrighteous still. For it is not what a man is not, but what a man does, that declares him a righteous man. Suppose a man be no thief, no liar, no unjust man; or, as the Pharisee saith, no extortioner, nor adulterer, &c., this will not make a righteous man; but there must be joined to these, holy and good actions, before he can be declared a righteous man.

Wherefore, as the apostle, when he pressed the Christians to righteousness, did put them first upon negative holiness, so he joineth thereto an exhortation to positive holiness; knowing, that where positive holiness is wanting, all the negative holiness in the whole world cannot declare a man a righteous man. When therefore he had said, "But thou, O man of God, flee these things" (sin and wickedness), he adds, "and follow after righteousness, godliness, faith, love, patience, meekness," &c.; 1 Tim. vi. 11. Here Timothy is exhorted to negative holiness, when he is bid to flee sin. Here also he is exhorted to positive holiness, when he is bid to follow after righteousness, &c.; for righteousness can neither stand in negative nor positive holiness, as severed one from another. That man then, and that man only, is, as to actions, a righteous man, that hath left off to do evil, and hath learned to do well, Isa. i. 16, 17; that hath cast off the works of darkness, and put on the armour of light. "Flee youthful lusts (said Paul), but follow righteousness, faith, charity, peace, with them that call on the Lord out of a pure heart;" 2 Tim. ii. 22.

The Pharisee, therefore, as to the general description of righteousness, made his definition right; but as to his person and personal righteousness, he made his definition wrong. I do not mean he defined his own righteousness wrong; but I mean his definition of true righteousness, which standeth in negative and positive holiness, he made to stoop to justify his own righteousness, and therein he played the hypocrite in his prayer: for although it is true righteousness that standeth in negative and positive holiness; yet that this is not true righteousness that standeth, but in some pieces and ragged remnants of negative and positive righteousness. If then the Pharisee would, in his definition of personal righteousness, have proved his own righteousness to be good, he must have proved, that both his negative and positive holiness had been universal; to wit, that he had left off to act in any wickedness, and that he had given up himself to the duty enjoined in every commandment: for so the righteous man is described; Job i. 8; ii. 3. As it is said of Zacharias and Elisabeth his wife, "They were both righteous before God, walking in all the commandments and ordinances of the Lord blameless;" Luke i. 5, 6. Here the perfection, that is, the universality, of their negative holiness is implied, and the universality of their positive holiness is expressed: they walked in all the commandments of the Lord; but that they could not do, if they had lived in any unrighteous thing or way. They walked in all blamelessly, that is, sincerely, with upright hearts. The Pharisee's righteousness, therefore, even by his own implied definition of righteousness, was not good, as is manifest these two ways -

1. His negative holiness was not universal.

2. His positive holiness was rather ceremonial than moral.

1. His negative holiness was not universal. He saith indeed, he was not an extortioner, nor unjust, no adulterer, nor yet as this Publican: but none of these expressions apart, nor all, if put together, do prove him to be perfect as to negative holiness; that is, they do not prove him, should it be granted, that he was as holy with this kind of holiness, as himself of himself had testified. For,

(1.) What though he was no extortioner, he might yet be a covetous man; Luke xvi. 14.

(2.) What though, as to dealing, he was not unjust to others, yet he wanted honesty to do justice to his own soul; Luke xvi. 15.

(3.) What though he was free from the act of adultery, he might yet be made guilty by an adulterous eye, against which the Pharisee did not watch (Matt. v. 28), of which the Pharisee did not take cognizance.

(4.) What though he was not like the Publican, yet he was like, yea was, a downright hypocrite; he wanted in those things wherein he boasted himself, sincerity; but without sincerity no action can be good, or accounted of God as righteous. The Pharisee, therefore, notwithstanding his boast, was deficient in his righteousness, though he would fain have shrouded it under the right definition thereof.

(5.) Nor doth his positive holiness help him at all, forasmuch as it is grounded mostly, if not altogether, in ceremonial holiness: nay, I will recollect myself, it was grounded partly in ceremonial and partly in superstitious holiness, if there be such a thing as superstitious holiness in the world; this paying of tithes was ceremonial, such as came in and went out with the typical priesthood. But what is that to positive holiness, when it was but a small pittance by the by. Had the Pharisee argued plainly and honestly; I mean, had he so dealt with that law, by which now he sought to be justified, he should have brought forth positive righteousness in morals, and should have said and proved it too, that as he was no wicked man with reference to the act of wickedness, he was indeed a righteous man in acts of moral virtues. He should, I say, have proved himself a true lover of God, no superstitious one, but a sincere worshipper of him; for this is contained in the first table (Exod. xx.), and is so in sum expounded by the Lord Christ himself (Mark xii. 30). He should also, in the next place, have proved himself truly kind, compassionate, liberal, and full of love and charity to his neighbour; for that is the sum of the second table, as our Lord doth expound it, saying, "Thou shalt love thy neighbour as thyself;" Mark xii. 31.

True, he says, he did them no hurt; but did he do them good? To do no hurt, is one thing; and to do good, is another; and it is possible for a man to do neither hurt nor good to his neighbour. What then, is he a righteous man because he hath done him no hurt? No, verily; unless, to his power, he hath also done him good.

It is therefore a very fallacious and deceitful arguing of the Pharisee, thus to speak before God in his prayers: I am righteous, because I have not hurt my neighbour, and because I have acted in ceremonial duties. Nor will that help him at all to say, he gave tithes of all that he possessed. It had been more modest to say, that he had paid them; for they, being commanded, were a due debt; nor could they go before God for a free gift, because, by the commandment, they were made a payment; but proud men and hypocrites love so to word it both with God and man, as at least to imply, that they are more forward to do, than God's command is to require them to do.

The second part of his positive holiness was superstitious; for God had appointed no such set fasts, neither more nor less but just twice a-week: "I fast twice a-week." Ay, but who did command thee to do so, other than by thy being put upon it by a superstitious and erroneous conscience, doth not, nor canst thou make to appear. This part, therefore, of this positive righteousness, was positive superstition, and abuse of God's law, and a gratification of thy own erroneous conscience. Hitherto, therefore, thou art defective in thy so seemingly brave and glorious righteousness.

Yet this let me say, in commendation of the Pharisee, in my conscience he was better than many of our English Christians; for many of them are so far off from being at all partakers of positive righteousness, that neither all their ministers, Bibles, and good books, good sermons, nor yet God's judgments, can persuade them to become so much as negatively holy, that is, to leave off evil.

The second thing that I take notice of in this prayer of the Pharisee, is his manner of delivery, as he stood praying in the temple: "God, I thank thee," said he, "that I am not as other men are." He seemed to be at this time in more than an ordinary frame, while now he stood in the presence of the divine Majesty: for a prayer made up of praise, is a prayer made up of the highest order, and is most like the way of them that are now in a state beyond prayer. Praise is the work of heaven; but we see here, that an hypocrite may get into that vein, even while an hypocrite, and while on earth below. Nor do I think that this prayer of his was a premeditated stinted form, but a prayer extempore, made on a sudden according to what he felt, thought, or understood of himself.

Here therefore we may see, that even prayer, as well as other acts of religious worship, may be performed in great hypocrisy; although I think, that to perform prayer in hypocrisy, is one of the most daring sins that are committed by the sons of men. For by prayer, above all duties, is our most direct and immediate personal approach into the presence of God; as there is an uttering of things before him, especially a giving to him of thanks for things received, or a begging that such and such things might be bestowed upon me. But now, to do these things in hypocrisy (and it is easy to do them so, when we go up into the temple to pray), must needs be intolerable wickedness, and it argueth infinite patience in God, that he should let such as do so arise alive from their knees, or that he should suffer them to go away from the place where they stand, without some token or mark of his wrath upon them.

I also observe, that this extempore prayer of the Pharisee was performed by himself, or in the strength of his own natural parts; for so the text implieth. "The Pharisee," saith the text, "stood and prayed thus with himself," or "by himself," and may signify, either that he spoke softly, or that he made this prayer by reason of his natural parts. "I will pray with the Spirit," said Paul; 1 Cor. xiv. 15. "The Pharisee prayed with himself," said Christ. It is at this day wonderfully common for men to pray extempore also; to pray by a book, by a premeditated set form, is now out of fashion. He is counted nobody now, that cannot at any time, at a minute's warning, make a prayer of half an hour long. I am not against extempore prayer, for I believe it to be the best kind of praying; but yet I am jealous, that there are a great many such prayers made, especially in pulpits and public meetings, without the breathing of the Holy Ghost in them; for if a Pharisee of old could do so, why not a Pharisee do the same now? Wit and reason, and notion, are not screwed up to a very great height; nor do men want words, or fancies, or pride, to make them do this thing. Great is the formality of religion this day, and little the power thereof. Now, where there is a great form, and little power (and such there was among the Jews, in the time of our Lord and Saviour Jesus Christ), there men are most strangely under the temptation to be hypocrites; for nothing doth so properly and directly oppose hypocrisy, as the power and glory of the things we profess. And so, on the contrary, nothing is a greater temptation to hypocrisy, than a form of knowledge of things without the savour thereof. Nor can much of the power and savour of the things of the gospel be seen at this day upon professors (I speak not now of all), if their notions and conversations be compared together. How proud, how covetous, how like the world in garb and guise, in words and actions, are most of the great professors of this our day! But when they come to divine worship, especially to pray, by their words and carriage there, one would almost judge them to be angels in heaven. But such things must be done in hypocrisy, as also the Pharisee's was.

"The Pharisee stood and prayed thus with himself."

And in that it is said he prayed with himself, it may signify, that he went in his prayer no further than his sense and reason, feeling and carnal apprehensions went. True Christian prayer ofttimes leaves sense and reason, feeling and carnal apprehensions, behind it; and it goeth forth with faith, hope, and desires to know what at present we are ignorant of, and that unto which our sense, feeling, reason, &c., are strangers. The apostle indeed doth say, "I will pray with the understanding;" 1 Cor. xiv. 15; but then it must be taken for an understanding spiritually enlightened. I say, it must be so understood, because the natural understanding, as such, receiveth not the things of God, therefore cannot pray for them; for they to such are foolish things; 1 Cor. ii. 14.

Now, a spiritually enlightened understanding may be officious in prayer these ways -

1. As it has received conviction of the truth of the being of the Spirit of God; for to receive conviction of the truth and being of such things, comes from the Spirit of God, not from the law, sense, or reason; 1 Cor. ii. 10-12. Now the understanding having, by the Holy Ghost, received conviction of the truth of things, draweth out the heart to cry in prayer to God for them. Therefore he saith, he would pray with the understanding.

2. The spiritually enlightened understanding hath also received, by the Holy Ghost, conviction of the excellency and glory of the things that are of the Spirit of

God, and so inflameth the heart with more fervent desires in this duty of prayer; for there is a supernatural excellency in the things that are of the Spirit: "For if the ministration of death (to which the Pharisee adhered), written and engraven in stones, was glorious, so that the children of Israel could not steadfastly behold the face of Moses, for the glory of his countenance, which glory was to be done away; how shall not the ministration of the Spirit be rather glorious? For if the ministration of condemnation be glory, much more doth the ministration of righteousness exceed in glory: for even that which was made glorious hath no glory in this respect, by reason of the glory that excelleth;" 2 Cor. iii. 7-10. And the Spirit of God sheweth, at least, some things of that excellent glory of them to the understanding that it enlighteneth; Eph. i. 17-19.

3. The spiritually enlightened understanding hath also thereby received knowledge, that these excellent supernatural things of the Spirit are given by covenant in Christ to those that love God, and are beloved of him. "Now we have received," says Paul, "not the spirit of the world (that the Pharisee had), but the Spirit which is of God, that we make know the things that are freely given to us of God;" 1 Cor. ii. 12. And this knowledge, that the things of the Spirit of God are freely given to us of God, puts yet a greater edge, more vigour, and yet further confidence, into the heart to ask for what is mine by gift, by a free gift of God in his Son. But all these things the poor Pharisee was an utter stranger to; he knew not the Spirit, nor the things of the Spirit, and therefore must neglect faith, judgment, and the love of God, Matt. xxiii. 23; Luke xi. 42, and follow himself only, as to his sense, feeling, reason, and carnal imagination in prayer.

He stood and prayed thus "with himself." He prayed thus, talking to himself; for so also it may (I think) be understood. It is said of the unjust judge, "he said within himself, Though I fear not God, nor regard man," &c., Luke xviii. 4; that is, he said it to himself. So the Pharisee is said to pray with himself: God and the Pharisee were not together, there was only the Pharisee and himself. Paul knew not what to pray for without the Holy Ghost joined himself with him, and helping him with groans unutterable; but the Pharisee had no need of that; it was enough that he and himself were together at this work; for he thought without doubting that he and himself together could do. How many times have I heard ancient men, and ancient women at it with themselves, when all alone in some private room, or in some solitary path; and in their chat they have been sometimes reasoning, sometimes chiding, sometimes pleading, sometimes praying, and sometimes singing; but yet all has been done by themselves when all alone; but yet so done, as one that has not seen them must needs have concluded that they were talking, singing, and praying with company, when all that they had said, they did it with themselves, and had neither auditor nor regarder.

So the Pharisee was at it with himself; he and himself performed, at this time, the duty of prayer. Now I observe, that usually when men do speak to or with themselves, they greatly strive to please themselves: therefore it is said, there is a man "that flattereth himself in his own eyes, until his iniquity be found to be hateful;" Psalm xxxvi. 2. He flattereth himself in his own way, according as his sense and carnal reason dictate to him; and he might do it as well in prayer as in any other way. Some men will so hear sermons and apply them that they may please themselves; and some men will pray, but will refuse such words and thoughts in prayer as will not please themselves.

O how many men speak all that they speak in prayer, rather to themselves, or to their auditory, than to God that dwelleth in heaven. And this I take to be the manner, I mean something of the manner, of the Pharisee's praying. Indeed, he made mention of God, as also others do; but he prayed with himself to himself, in his own spirit, and to his own pleasing, as the matter of his prayer doth manifest. For was it not pleasant to this hypocrite, think you, to speak thus well of himself at this time? Doubtless it was. Also children and fools are of the same temper with hypocrites, as to this: they also love, without ground, as the Pharisee, to flatter themselves in their own eyes; "But not he that commendeth himself is approved."

"God, I thank thee, I am not as other men are, extortioners, unjust, adulterers, or even as this Publican," &c.

Thus he begins his prayer; and it is, as was hinted before, a prayer of the highest strain. For to make a prayer all of thanksgiving, and to urge in that prayer the cause of that thanksgiving, is the highest manner of praying, and seems to be done in the strongest faith, &c., in the greatest sense of things. And such was the Pharisee's prayer, only he wanted substantial ground for his thanksgiving; to wit, he wanted proof of that he said, He was not as other men were, except he had meant, he did not, that he was even of the worst sort of men: For even the best of men by nature, and the worst, are all alike. "What, then, are we better than they? (saith Paul), No, in nowise;" Rom. iii. 9. So then he failed in the ground of his thankfulness, and therefore his thankfulness was grounded on untruth, and so became feigned and self-flattering, and could not be acceptable with the God of heaven.

Besides, in this high prayer of the Pharisee, he fathered that upon God which he could by no means own; to wit, that he being so good as he thought himself to be, was through distinguishing love and favour of God--"God, I thank thee, that I am not as other men are." I thank thee, that thou hast made me better than others; I thank thee that my condition is so good, and that I am so far advanced above my neighbour.

There are several things flow from this prayer of the Pharisee that are worth our observation: as -

1. That the Pharisees and hypocrites do not love to count themselves sinners, when they stand before God.

They choose rather to commend themselves before him for virtuous and holy persons, sometimes saying, and oftener thinking, that they are more righteous than others. Yea, it seems by the word to be natural, hereditary, and so common for hypocrites to trust to themselves that they are righteous, and then to condemn others: this is the foundation upon which this very parable is built: "He spake this parable (saith Luke) unto certain which trusted in themselves as being righteous," or "that they were" so, "and despised others," ver. 9.

I say, hypocrites love not to think of their sins, when they stand in the presence of God; but rather to muster up, and to present him with their several good deeds, and to venture a standing or falling by them.

2. This carriage of the Pharisee before God informs us, that moral virtues, and the ground of them, which is the law, if trusted to, blinds the mind of man that he cannot for them perceive the way to happiness. While Moses is read (and his law and the righteousness thereof trusted to), the vail is upon their heart; and even unto this day (said Paul) the vail remaineth "untaken away in the reading of the Old Testament, which vail is done away in Christ. But even unto this day, when Moses is read, the vail is upon their heart;" 2 Cor. iii. 14, 15. And this is the reason so many moral men, that are adorned with civil and moral righteousness, are yet so ignorant of themselves, and the way of life by Christ.

The law of works, and the righteousness of the flesh, which is the righteousness of the law, blinds their minds, shuts up their eyes, and causeth them to miss of the righteousness that they are so hotly in the pursuit of. Their minds were blinded, saith the text. Whose minds? Why those that adhered to, that stood by, and that sought righteousness of the law. Now,

The Pharisee was such an one; he rested in the law, he made his boast of God, and trusted to himself that he was righteous; all this proceeded of that blindness and ignorance that the law had possessed his mind withal; for it is not granted to the law to be the ministration of life and light, but to be the ministration of death, when it speaks; and of darkness, when trusted unto, that the Son of God might have the pre-eminence in all things: therefore it is said when the heart "shall turn to him, the vail shall be taken away;" 2 Cor. iii. 16.

3. We may see by this prayer, the strength of vain confidence; it will embolden a man to stand in a lie before God; it will embolden a man to trust to himself, and to what he hath done; yea, to plead his own goodness, instead of God's mercy, before him. For the Pharisee was not only a man that justified himself before men, but that justified himself before God; and what was the cause of his so justifying himself before God, but that vain confidence that he had in himself and his works, which were both a cheat and a lie to himself? But I say, the boldness of the man was wonderful, for he stood to the lie that was in his right hand, and pleaded the goodness of it before him.

But besides these things, there are four things more that are couched in this prayer of the Pharisee.

1. By this prayer the Pharisee doth appropriate to himself conversion; he challengeth it to himself and to his fellows. "I am not," saith he, "as other men;" that is, in unconversion, in a state of sin, wrath, and death: and this must be his meaning, for the religion of the Pharisee was not grounded upon any particular natural privilege: I mean not singly, not only upon that, but upon a falling in with those principles, notions, opinions, decrees, traditions, and doctrines that they taught distinct from the true and holy doctrines of the prophets. And they made to themselves disciples by such doctrine, men that they could captivate by those principles, laws, doctrines, and traditions: and therefore such are said to be of the sect of the Pharisees: that is, the scholars and disciples of them, converted to them and to their doc-

trine. O! it is easy for souls to appropriate conversion to themselves, that know not what conversion is. It is easy, I say, for men to lay conversion to God, on a legal, or ceremonial, or delusive bottom, on such a bottom that will sink under the burden that is laid upon it; on such a bottom that will not stand when it is brought under the touchstone of God, nor against the rain, wind, and floods that are ordained to put it to the trial, whether it is true or false. The Pharisee here stands upon a supposed conversion to God; "I am not as other men;" but both he and his conversion are rejected by the sequel of the parable: "That which is highly esteemed among men" (Luke xvi. 15) "is abomination in the sight of God." That is, that conversion, that men, as men, flatter themselves that they have, is such. But the Pharisee will be a converted man, he will have more to shew for heaven than his neighbour--"I am not as other men are;" to wit, in a state of sin and condemnation, but in a state of conversion and salvation. But see how grievously this sect, this religion, beguiled men. It made them twofold worse the children of hell than they were before, and than their teachers were, Matth. xxiii. 15; that is, their doctrine begat such blindness, such vain confidence, and groundless boldness in their disciples, as to involve them in that conceit of conversion that was false, and so if trusted to, damnable.

2. By these words, we find the Pharisee, not only appropriating conversion to himself, but rejoicing in that conversion: "God, I thank thee," saith he, "that I am not as other men;" which saying of his gives us to see that he gloried in his conversion; he made no doubt at all of his state, but lived in the joy of the safety that he supposed his soul, by his conversion, to be in. Oh! thanks to God, says he, I am not in the state of sin, death, and damnation, as the unjust, and this Publican is. What a strange delusion, to trust to the spider's web, and to think that a few, or the most fine of the works of the flesh, would be sufficient to bear up the soul in, at, and under the judgment of God! "There is a generation that are pure in their own eyes, and yet are not washed from their filthiness." This text can be so fitly applied to none as the Pharisee, and to those that tread in the Pharisee's steps, and that are swallowed up with his conceits, and with the glory of their own righteousness.

So again, "There is a way" (a way to heaven) "which seemeth right to a man, but the end thereof are the ways of death;" Prov. xxx. 12; xiv. 12. This also is fulfilled in these kind of men; at the end of their way is death and hell, notwithstanding their confidence in the goodness of their state.

Again, "There is that maketh himself rich, yet hath nothing;" Prov. xiii. 7. What can be more plain from all these texts, than that some men that are out of the way think themselves in it; and that some men think themselves clean, that are yet in their filthiness, and that think themselves rich for the next world, and yet are poor, and miserable, and wretched, and blind, and naked. Thus the poor, blind, naked, hypocritical Pharisee thought of himself, when God threatened to abase him: yea, he thought himself thus, and joyed therein, when indeed he was going down to the chambers of death.

3. By these words, the Pharisee seems to put the goodness of his condition upon the goodness of God. I am not as other men are, and I thank God for it. "God (saith he), I thank thee, that I am not as other men are." He thanked God, when God had done nothing for him. He thanked God, when the way that he was in was not of God's prescribing, but of his own inventing. So the persecutor thanks God that he was put into that way of roguery that the devil had put him into, when he fell to rending and tearing of the church of God; "Their possessors slay them (saith the prophet), and hold themselves not guilty: and they that sell them say, Blessed be the Lord, for I am rich;" Zech. xi. 5. I remember that Luther used to say, "In the name of God begins all mischief." All must be fathered upon God: the Pharisee's conversion must be fathered upon God; the right, or rather the villany of the outrageous persecution against God's people, must be fathered upon God. "God, I thank thee," and, "Blessed be God," must be the burden of the heretic's song. So again, the free-willer, he will ascribe all to God; the Quaker, the Ranter, the Socinian, &c., will ascribe all to God. "God, I thank thee," is in every man's mouth, and must be entailed to every error, delusion, and damnable doctrine that is in the world: but the name of God, and their doctrine, worship, and way, hangeth together, as the Pharisee's doctrine; that is to say, by nothing at all: for God hath not proposed their principles, nor doth he own them, nor hath he commanded them, nor doth he convey by them the least grace or mercy to them; but rather rejecteth them, and holdeth them for his enemies, and for the destroyers of the world.

4. We come, in the next place, to the ground of all this, and that is, to what the Pharisee had attained; to wit, that he was no extortioner, no unjust man, no adulterer, nor even as this Publican, and for that he fasted twice a-week, and paid tithes of all that he possessed. So that you see he pretended to a double foundation for

his salvation, a moral and a ceremonial one; but both very lean, weak, and feeble: for the first of his foundation, what is it more, if all be true that he saith, but a being removed a few inches from the vilest men in their vilest actions? a very slender matter to build my confidence for heaven upon.

And for the second part of his ground for life, what is it but a couple of ceremonies, if so good? the first is questioned as a thing not founded in God's law; and the second is such, as is of the remotest sort of ceremonies, that teach and preach the Lord Jesus. But suppose them to be the best, and his conformity to them the thoroughest, they never were ordained to get to heaven by, and so are become but a sandy foundation. But any thing will serve some men for a foundation and support for their souls, and to build their hopes of heaven upon. I am not a drunkard, says one, nor a liar, nor a swearer, nor a thief, and therefore I thank God, I have hopes of heaven and glory. I am not an extortioner, nor an adulterer; not unjust, nor yet as this Publican; and therefore do hope I shall go to heaven. Alas, poor men! will your being furnished with these things save you from the thundering claps and vehement batteries that the wrath of God will make upon sin and sinners in the day that shall burn like an oven? No, no; nothing at that day can shroud a man from the hot rebukes of that vengeance, but the very righteousness of God, which is not the righteousness of the law, however christened, named, or garnished with all the righteousness of man.

But, O thou blind Pharisee! since thou art so confident that thy state is good, and thy righteousness is that that will stand when it shall be tried with fire (1 Cor. iii. 13), let me now reason with thee of righteousness. My terror shall not make thee afraid; I am not God, but a man as thou art; we both are formed out of the clay.

First, Prithee, when didst thou begin to be righteous? Was it before or after thou hadst been a sinner? Not before, I dare say; but if after, then the sins that thou pollutedst thyself withal before, have made thee incapable of acting legal righteousness: for sin, where it is, pollutes, defiles, and makes vile the whole man; therefore thou canst not by after acts of obedience make thyself just in the sight of that God thou pretendest now to stand praying unto. Indeed thou mayst cover thy dirt, and paint thy sepulchre; for that acts of after obedience will do, though sin has gone before. But, Pharisee, God can see through the white of this wall, even to the dirt that is within: God can also see through the paint and garnish of thy beauteous sepulchre, to the dead men's bones that are within; nor can any of thy most holy duties, nor all when put together, blind the eye of the all-seeing Majesty from beholding all the uncleanness of thy soul (Matt. xxiii. 27.) Stand not therefore so stoutly to it, now thou art before God; sin is with thee, and judgment and justice is before him. It becomes thee, therefore, rather to despise and abhor this life, and to count all thy doings but dross and dung, and to be content to be justified with another's righteousness instead of thy own. This is the way to be secured. I say, blind Pharisee, this is the way to be secured from the wrath which is to come.

There is nothing more certain than this, that as to justification from the curse of the law, God has rejected man's righteousness, for the weakness and unprofitableness thereof, and hath accepted in the room of that the glorious righteousness of his Son; because indeed that, and that only, is universal, perfect, and equal with his justice and holiness. This is in a manner the contents of the whole Bible, and therefore must needs be more certainly true. Now then, Mr Pharisee, methinks, what if thou didst this, and that while thou art at thy prayers, to wit, cast in thy mind what doth God love most? and the resolve will be at hand. The best righteousness, surely the best righteousness; for that thy reason will tell thee: This done, even while thou art at thy devotion, ask thyself again, But who has the best righteousness? and that resolve will be at hand also; to wit, he that in person is equal with God, and that is his in Jesus Christ; he that is separate from sinners, and made higher than the heavens, and that is his Son Jesus Christ; he that did no sin, nor had any guile found in his mouth; and there never was any such he in all the world but the Son of God, Jesus Christ.

Now, Pharisee, when thou hast done this, then, as thou art at thy devotion, ask again, But what is this best righteousness, the righteousness of Christ, to do? and the answer will be ready. It is to be made by an act of the sovereign grace of God over to the sinner that shall dare to trust thereto for justification from the curse of the law. "He is made unto us of God, righteousness." "He hath made him to be sin for us, who knew no sin; that we might be made the righteousness of God in him." "For Christ is the end of the law for righteousness to every one that believeth;" 1 Cor. i. 30; 2 Cor. v. 21; Rom. x. 4.

This done, and concluded on, then turn again, Pharisee, and say thus with thyself--Is it most safe for me to trust in this righteousness of God, this righteousness of God-man, this righteousness of Christ? Certainly it is; since, by the text, it is counted the best, and that which is best pleaseth God; since it is that which God hath appointed, that sinners shall be justified withal. For "in the Lord have we righteousness" if we believe: and, "in the Lord we are justified, and do glory;" Isa. xlv. 24, 25.

Nay, Pharisee, suppose thine own righteousness should be as long, as broad, as high, as deep, as perfect, as good, even every way as good, as the righteousness of Christ; yet since God has chosen, by Christ, to reconcile us to himself, canst thou attempt to seek by thy own righteousness to reconcile thyself to God, and not attempt (at least) to confront this righteousness of Christ before God; yea, to challenge it by acceptance of thy person contrary to God's design?

Suppose, that when the king has chosen one to be judge in the land, and has determined that he shall be judge in all cases, and that by his verdict every man's judgment shall stand; I say, suppose, after this, another should arise, and of his own head resolve to do his own business himself. Now, though he should be every whit as able, yea, and suppose he should do it as justly and righteously too, yet his making of himself a judge, would be an affront to the king, and an act of rebellion, and so a transgression worthy of punishment.

Why, Pharisee, God hath appointed, that by the righteousness of his Son, and by that righteousness only, men shall be justified in his sight from the curse of the law. Wherefore, take heed, and at thy peril, whatever thy righteousness is, confront not the righteousness of Christ therewith. I say, bring it not in, let it not plead for thee at the bar of God, nor do thou plead for that in his court of justice; for thou canst not do this and be innocent. If he trust to his righteousness, he hath sinned, says Ezekiel. Mark the text, "When I shall say to the righteous, that he shall surely live; if he trust to his own righteousness, and commit iniquity, all his righteousness shall not be remembered: but for his iniquity that he hath committed, he shall die for it;" Ezek. xxxiii. 13.

Observe a few things from this text; and they are these that follow.

1. Here is a righteous man; a man with whom we do not hear that the God of heaven finds fault.

2. Here is a promise made to this man, that he shall surely live; but on this condition, that he trust not to his own righteousness. Whence it is manifest, that

the promise of life to this righteous man, is not for the sake of his righteousness, but for the sake of something else; to wit, the righteousness of Christ.

1. Not for the sake of his own righteousness. This is evident, because we are permitted, yea, commanded, to trust in the righteousness that saveth us. The righteousness of God is unto us all, and upon all that believe; that is, trust in it, and trust to it for justification. Now therefore, if thy righteousness, when most perfect, could save thee, thou mightst, yea oughtst, most boldly to trust therein. But since thou art forbidden to trust to it, it is evident it cannot save; nor is it for the sake of that, that the righteous man is saved; Rom. iii. 21, 22.

2. But for the sake of something else, to wit, for the sake of the righteousness of Christ, "Whom God hath set forth to be a propitiation through faith in his blood, to declare his righteousness for the remission of sins that are past, through the forbearance of God; to declare, I say, at this time his righteousness, that he might be just, and the justifier of him that believeth in Jesus;" Rom. iii. 25, 26; see Phil. iii. 6-8.

"If he trust to his own righteousness, and commit iniquity, all his righteousness shall not be remembered; but for his iniquity that he hath committed (in trusting to his own righteousness), he shall die for it."

Note hence further.

1. That there is more virtue in one sin to destroy, than in all thy righteousness to save thee alive. If he trust, if he trust ever so little, if he do at all trust to his own righteousness, all his righteousness shall be forgotten; and by, and for, and in, the sin that he hath committed, in trusting to it, he shall die.

2. Take notice also, that there are more damnable sins than those that are against the moral law. By which of the ten commandments is trusting to our own righteousness forbidden? Yet it is a sin: it is a sin therefore forbidden by the gospel, and is included, lurketh close in, yea, is the very root of, unbelief itself; "He that believes not shall be damned." But he that trusteth in his own righteousness doth not believe, neither in the truth, nor sufficiency of the righteousness of Christ to save him, therefore he shall be damned.

But how is it manifest, that he that trusteth to his own righteousness, doth it through a doubt, or unbelief of the truth or sufficiency of the righteousness of Christ?

I answer, because he trusteth to his own. A man will never willingly choose to trust to the worst of helps, when he believes there is a better as near, and to be had as soon, and that too, upon as easy, if not more easy terms. If he that trusteth to his own righteousness for life, did believe that there is indeed such a thing as the righteousness of Christ to justify, and that this righteousness of Christ has in it all-sufficiency to do that blessed work, be sure he would choose that, thereon to lay, lean, and venture his soul, that he saw was the best, and most sufficient to save; especially when he saw also (and see that he must, when he sees the righteousness of Christ), to wit, that that is to be obtained as soon, because as near, and to be had on as easy terms: nay, upon easier than man's own righteousness. I say, he would sooner choose it, because of the weight of salvation, of the worth of salvation, and of the fearful sorrow that to eternity will overtake him that in this thing shall miscarry. It is for heaven, it is to escape hell, wrath, and damnation, saith the soul; and therefore I will, I must, I dare not but choose that, and that only, that I believe to be the best and most sufficient help in so great a concern as soul-concern is. So then he that trusteth to his own righteousness, does it of unbelief of the sufficiency of the righteousness of Christ to save him.

Wherefore this sin of trusting to his own righteousness is a most high transgression; because it contemneth the righteousness of Christ, which is the only righteousness that is sufficient to save from the curse of the law. It also disalloweth the design of heaven, and the excellency of the mystery of the wisdom of God, in designing this way of salvation for man. What shall I say, It also seeketh to rob God of the honour of the salvation of man. It seeketh to take the crown from the head of Christ, and to set it upon the hypocrite's head; therefore, no marvel that this one sin be of that weight, virtue, and power, as to sink that man and his righteousness into hell, that leaneth thereon, or trusteth unto it.

But, Pharisee, I need not talk thus unto thee; for thou art not the man that hath that righteousness that God findeth not fault withal; nor is it to be found, but with him that is ordained to be the Saviour of mankind; nor is there any such one besides Jesus, who is called Christ. What madness then has brought thee into the temple, there in an audacious manner to stand and vaunt before God, saying, "God, I thank thee, I am not as other men are?"

Dost thou not know, that he that breaks one, breaks all the commandments of God; and consequently, that he that keeps not all, keeps none at all of the commandments of God? Saith not the scripture the same? "For whosoever shall keep the whole law, and yet offend in one point, he is guilty of all;" Jam. ii. 10. Be confounded then, be confounded.

Dost thou know the God with whom now thou hast to do? He is a God that cannot (as he is just) accept of an half righteousness for a whole; of a lame righteousness for a sound; of a sick righteousness for a well and healthy one; Mal. i. 7, 8. And if so, how should he then accept of that which is no righteousness? I say, how should he accept of that which is none at all, for thine is only such? And if Christ said, "When you have done all, say, We are unprofitable," how camest thou to say, before thou hadst done one thing well, I am better, more righteous than other men?

Didst thou believe, when thou saidst it, that God knew thy heart? Hadst thou said this to the Publican, it had been a high and rampant expression; but to say this before God, to the face of God, when he knew that thou wert vile, and a sinner from the womb, and from the conception, spoils all. It was spoken to put a check to thy arrogancy when Christ said, "Ye are they that justify yourselves before men; but God knoweth your hearts;" Luke xvi. 15.

Hast thou taken notice of this, that God judgeth the fruit by the heart from whence it comes? "A good man, out of the good treasure of his heart, bringeth forth that which is good; and an evil man, out of the evil treasure of his heart, bringeth forth that which is evil;" Luke vi. 45. Nor can it be otherwise concluded, but that thou art an evil man, and so that all thy supposed good is nought but badness; for that thou hast made it to stand in the room of Jesus, and hast dared to commend thyself to the living God thereby: for thou hast trusted in thy shadow of righteousness, and committed iniquity. Thy sin hath melted away thy righteousness, and turned it to nothing but dross; or, if you will, to the early dew, like to which it goeth away, and so can by no means do thee good, when thou shalt stand in need of salvation and eternal life of God.

But, further, thou sayst thou art righteous; but they are but vain words. Knowest thou not that thy zeal, which is the life of thy righteousness, is preposterous in many things? What else means thy madness, and the rage thereof, against men as good as thyself. True, thy being ignorant that they are good, may save thee from the commission of the sin that is unpardonable; but it will never keep thee from spot in

God's sight, but will make both thee and thy righteousness culpable.

Paul, who was once as brave a Pharisee as thou canst be, calleth much of that zeal which he in that estate was possessed with, and lived in the exercise of, madness; yea, exceeding madness (Acts xxvi. 9-11; Phil, iii. 5, 6); and of the same sort is much of thine, and it must be so; for a lawyer, a man for the law, and that resteth in it, must be a persecutor; yea, a persecutor of righteous men, and that of zeal to God; because by the law is begotten, through the weakness that it meeteth with in thee, sourness, bitterness of spirit, and anger against him that rightfully condemneth thee of folly, for choosing to trust to thy own righteousness when a better is provided of God to save us; Gal. iv. 28-31. Thy righteousness therefore is deficient; yea, thy zeal for the law, and the men of the law, has joined madness with thy moral virtues, and made thy righteousness unrighteousness: how then canst thou be upright before the Lord?

Further, has not the pride of thy spirit in this hotheaded zeal for thy Pharisaical notions run thee upon thinking that thou art able to do more than God hath enjoined thee, and so able to make thyself more righteous than God requireth thou shouldst be? What else is the cause of thy adding laws to God's laws, precepts to God's precepts, and traditions to God's appointment? Mark vii. Nay, hast thou not, by thus doing, condemned the law of want of perfection, and so the God that gave it, of want of wisdom and faithfulness to himself and thee?

Nay, I say again, hath not thy thus doing charged God with being ignorant of knowing what rules there needed to be imposed on his creatures to make their obedience complete? And doth not this madness of thine intimate, moreover, that if thou hadst not stepped in with the bundle of thy traditions, righteousness had been imperfect, not through man's weakness, but through impediment in God, or in his ministering rules of righteousness unto us?

Now, when thou hast thought on these things, fairly answer thyself these few questions. Is not this arrogancy? Is not this blasphemy? Is not this to condemn God, that thou mightst be righteous? And dost thou think, this is indeed the way to be righteous?

But again, what means thy preferring of thine own rules, laws, statutes, ordinances, and appointments, before the rules, laws, statutes, and appointments of God? Thinkest thou this to be right? Whither will thy zeal, thy pride, and thy folly carry thee? Is there more reason, more equity, more holiness in thy tradition, than in the holy, and just, and good commandments of God? Rom. vii. 12. Why then, I say, dost thou reject the commandment of God, to keep thine own tradition? Yea, why dost thou rage, and rail, and cry out, when men keep not thy law, or the rule of thine order, and tradition of thine elders, and yet shut thine eyes, or wink with them, when thou thyself shalt live in the breach of the law of God? Yea, why wilt thou condemn men, when they keep not thy law, but study for an excuse, yea, plead for them that live in the breach of God's? Mark vii. 10-13. Will this go for righteousness in the day of God Almighty? Nay, rather, will not this, like a mill-stone about thy neck, drown thee in the deeps of hell? O the blindness, the madness, the pride, that dwells in the hearts of these pretended righteous men

Again, What kind of righteousness of thine is this that standeth in a mis-esteeming of God's commands? Some thou settest too high, and some too low; as in the text, thou hast set a ceremony above faith, above love, and above hope in the mercy of God; when as it is evident, the things last mentioned, are the things of the first rate, the weightier matters; Matt. xxiii. 17.

Again, Thou hast preferred the gold above the temple that sanctifieth the gold; and the gift above the altar that sanctifieth the gift; Matt. xxiii. 17.

I say again, What kind of righteousness shall this be called? What back will such a suit of apparel fit, that is set together to what it should be? Nor can other righteousness proceed, where a wrong judgment precedeth it.

This misplacing of God's laws cannot, I say, but produce misplaced obedience. It indeed produceth a monster, an ill-shaped thing, unclean, and an abomination to the Lord. For "see," saith he (if thou wilt be making), "that thou make all things according to the pattern shewn thee in the mount." Set faith, where faith should stand; a moral, where a moral should stand; and a ceremony, where a ceremony should stand: for this turning of things upside down shall be esteemed as the potter's clay. And wilt thou call this thy righteousness? yea, wilt thou stand in this? wilt thou plead for this? and venture an eternal concern in such a piece of linsey-woolsey as this? O fools, and blind!

But, further, let us come a little closer to the point. O blind Pharisee, thou standest to thy righteousness: what dost thou mean? Wouldst thou have mercy for thy righteousness, or justice for thy righteousness.

If mercy, what mercy? Temporal things God giveth to the unthankful and unholy: nor doth he use to sell the world to man for righteousness. The earth hath he given to the children of men. But this is not the thing: thou wouldst have eternal mercy for thy righteousness; thou wouldst have God think upon what an holy, what a good, what a righteous man thou art and hast been. But Christ died not for the good and righteous, nor did he come to call such to the banquet that grace hath prepared for the world. "I came not,--I am not come (saith Christ) to call the righteous, but sinners to repentance;" Mark ii.; Rom. v. Yet this is thy plea; Lord, God, I am a righteous man; therefore grant me mercy, and a share in thy heavenly kingdom. What else dost thou mean when thou sayst, "God I thank thee, that I am not as other men are?" Why dost thou rejoice, why art thou glad that thou art more righteous (if indeed thou art) than thy neighbour, if it is not because thou thinkest that thou hast got the start of thy neighbour, with reference to mercy; and that by thy righteousness thou hast insinuated thyself into God's affections, and procured an interest in his eternal favour? But,

What, what hast thou done by thy righteousness? I say, What hast thou given to God thereby? And what hath he received of thy hand? Perhaps thou wilt say, righteousness pleaseth God: but I answer no, not thine, with respect to justification from the curse of the law, unless it be as perfect as the justice it is yielded to, and as the law that doth command it. But thine is not such a righteousness: no, thine is speckled, thine is spotted, thine makes thee to look like a speckled bird in his eye-sight.

Thy righteousness has added iniquity, because it has kept thee from a belief of thy need of repentance, and because it has emboldened thee to thrust thyself audaciously into the presence of God, and made thee even before his holy eyes, which are so pure, that they cannot look on iniquity (Hab. i. 13), to vaunt, boast, and brag of thyself; and of thy tottering, ragged, stinking uncleanness; for all our righteousnesses are as menstruous rags, because they flow from a thing, a heart, a man, that is unclean. But,

Again, Wouldst thou have mercy for thy righteousness? For whom wouldst thou have it: for another, or for thyself? If for another (and it is most proper that a righteous man should intercede for another by his righteousness, rather than for himself), then thou thrustest Christ out of his place and office, and makest thyself to be a saviour in his stead; for a mediator there is already, even a mediator between God and man, and he is the man Christ Jesus.

But dost thou plead by thy righteousness for mercy for thyself? Why, in doing so, thou impliest -

1. That thy righteousness can prevail with God more than can thy sins; I say, that thy righteousness can prevail with God to preserve thee from death more than thy sins can prevail with him to condemn thee to it. And if so, what follows, but that thy righteousness is more, and has been done in a fuller spirit than ever were thy sins? But thus to insinuate, is to insinuate a lie; for there is no man but, while he is a sinner, sinneth with a more full spirit than a good man can act righteousness withal.

A sinner, when he sinneth, he doth it with all his heart, and with all his mind, and with all his soul, and with all his strength; nor hath he in his ordinary course any thing that bindeth. But with a good man it is not so; all and every whit of himself, neither is, nor can be, in every good duty that he doth. For when he would do good, evil is the Spirit, and the Spirit against the flesh, and these are present with him. And again, "The flesh lusteth against one to the other, so that ye cannot do the things would;" Gal. v. 17.

Now, if a good man cannot do good things with that oneness and universalness of mind, as a wicked man doth sin with, then is his sin heavier to weigh him down to hell than is his righteousness to buoy him up to the heavens.

And again, I say, if the righteousness of a good man comes short of his sin, both in number, weight, and measure, as it doth (for a good man shrinks and quakes at the thoughts of God's entering into judgment with him, Psalm cxliii. 2); then is his iniquity more than his righteousness. And I say again, if the sin of one that is truly gracious, and so of one that hath the best of principles, is heavier and mightier to destroy him than is his righteousness to save him, how can it be that the Pharisee, that is not gracious, but a mere carnal man (somewhat reformed and painted over with a few lean and low formalities), should with his empty, partial, hypocritical righteousness counterpoise his great, mighty, and weighty sins, that have cleaved to him in every state and condition of his, to make him odious in the sight of God?

2. Dost thou plead by thy righteousness for mercy for thyself? Why in so doing thou impliest, that mercy thou deservest; and that is next door to, or almost as

much as to say, God oweth me what I ask for. The best that can be put upon it is, thou seekest security from the direful curse of God, as it were by the works of the law, Rom. ix. 31-33; and to be sure, betwixt Christ and the law, thou wilt drop into hell. For he that seeks for mercy, as it were, and but as it were, by the works of the law, doth not altogether trust thereto. Nor doth he that seeks for that righteousness that should save him as it were by the works of the law, seek it only wholly and solely at the hands of mercy.

So then, to seek for that that should save thee, neither at the hands of the law, nor at the hands of mercy, is to be sure to seek it where it is not to be found; for there is no medium betwixt the righteousness of the law and the mercy of God. Thou must have it either at the door of the law, or at the door of grace. But sayst thou, I am for having of it at the hands of both. I will trust solely to neither. I love to have two strings to my bow. If one of them, as you think, can help me by itself, my reason tells me that both can help me better. Therefore will I be righteous and good, and will seek by my goodness to be commended to the mercy of God: for surely he that hath something of his own to ingratiate himself into the favour of his prince withal, shall sooner obtain his mercy and favour, than one that comes to him stripped of all good.

I answer, But there are not two ways to heaven: there is but one new and living way which Christ hath consecrated for us through the vail, that is to say, his flesh; and besides that one, there is no more; Heb. x. 19-24. Why then dost thou talk of two strings to thy bow? What became of him that had, and would have two stools to sit on? yea, the text says plainly, that therefore they obtained not righteousness, because they sought it not by faith, but as it were by the works of the law. See here, they are disowned by the gospel, because they sought it not by faith, that is, by faith only. Again, the law, and the righteousness thereof, flies from them (nor could they attain it, though they follow after it), because they sought it not by faith.

Mercy then is to be found alone in Jesus Christ. Again, the righteousness of the law is to be obtained only by faith of Jesus Christ; that is, in the Son of God is the righteousness of the law to be found; for he, by his obedience to his Father, is become the end of the law for righteousness. And for the sake of his legal righteousness (which is also called the righteousness of God, because it was God in the flesh of the Lord Jesus that did accomplish it), is mercy, and grace from God extended to whoever dependeth by faith upon God by this Jesus his righteousness for it. And hence it is, that we so often read, that this Jesus is the way to the Father; that God, for Christ's sake, forgiveth us; that by the obedience of one many are made righteous, or justified; and that through this man is preached to us the forgiveness of sins; and that by him all that believe are justified from all things from which they could not be justified by the law of Moses.

Now, though I here do make mention of righteousness and mercy, yet I hold there is but one way, to wit, to eternal life; which way, as I said, is Jesus Christ; for he is the new, the only new and living way to the Father of mercies, for mercy to make me capable of abiding with him in the heavens for ever and ever.

But sayst thou, I will be righteous in myself that I may have wherewith to commend me to God, when I go to him for mercy?

I answer, But thou blind Pharisee, I tell thee thou hast no understanding of God's design by the gospel, which is, not to advance man's righteousness, as thou dreamest, but to advance the righteousness of his Son, and his grace by him. Indeed, if God's design by the gospel was to exalt and advance man's righteousness, then that which thou hast said would be to the purpose; for what greater dignity can be put upon man's righteousness, than to admit it?

I say then, for God to admit it, to be an advocate, an intercessor, a mediator; for all these are they which prevail with God to shew me mercy. But this God never thought of, much less could he thus design by the gospel; for the text runs flat against it. Not of works, not of works of righteousness, which we have done; "Not of works, lest any man should boast," saying, Well, I may thank my own good life for mercy. It was partly for the sake of my own good deeds that I obtained mercy to be in heaven and glory. Shall this be the burden of the song of heaven? or is this that which is composed by that glittering heavenly host, and which we have read of in the holy book of God? No, no; that song runs upon other feet--standeth in far better strains, being composed of far higher and truly heavenly matter: for God has "predestinated us unto the adoption of children by Jesus Christ to himself, according to the good pleasure of his will, to the praise of the glory of his grace, wherein he hath made us accepted in the Beloved: in whom we have redemption through his blood, the forgiveness of sins, according to the riches of his grace;" Eph. i. And it is requisite that the song be framed accordingly; wherefore he saith, that the heavenly song runs thus-- "Thou art worthy to take the book, and to open the seals thereof; for thou wast slain, and hast redeemed us to God by thy blood, out of every kindred, and tongue, and people, and nation; and hast made us unto our God kings and priests; and we shall reign on the earth;" Rev. v. 9, 10.

He saith not that they have redeemed, or helped to redeem and deliver them-selves; but that the Lamb, the Lamb that was slain; the Lamb only was he that re-deemed them. Nor, saith he, that they had made themselves kings and priests unto God to offer any oblation, sacrifice, or offering whatsoever, but that the same Lamb had made them such: for they, as is insinuated by the text, were in, among, one with, and no better than the kindreds, tongues, nations, and people of the earth. Better! "No, in no wise," saith Paul (Rom. iii. 9); therefore their separation from them was of mere mercy, free grace, good will, and distinguishing love; not for, or because of works of righteousness which any of them have done; no, they were all alike. But these, because beloved when in their blood (according to Ezek. xvi.), were separated by free grace; and as another scripture hath it, "redeemed from the earth," and from among men by blood; Rev. xiv. 3, 4. Wherefore deliverance from the ireful wrath of God must not, neither in whole nor in part, be ascribed to the whole law, or to all the righteousness that comes by it, but to this Lamb of God, Jesus, the Saviour of the world; for it is he that delivered us from the wrath to come, and that according to God's appointment; "for God hath not appointed us to wrath, but to obtain salvation by (or through) our Lord Jesus Christ;" 1 Thess. i. 10; v. 9. Let every man, therefore, take heed what he doth, and whereon he layeth the stress of his salvation; "For other foundation can no man lay than that is laid, which is Jesus Christ;" 1 Cor. iii. ii.

But dost thou plead still as thou didst before, and wilt thou stand thereto? Why then, thy design must overcome God, or God's design must overcome thee. Thy design is to give thy good life, thy good deeds, a part of the glory of thy justifica-tion from the curse. And God's design is to throw all thy righteousness out into the street, into the dirt and dunghill, as to that thou art for glory, and for glorying here before God; yea, thou art sharing in the glory of justification when that alone belongeth to God. And he hath said, "My glory will I not give to another." Thou wilt not trust wholly to God's grace in Christ for justification; and God will not take thy stinking righteousness in as a partner in thy acquitment from sin, death, wrath, and hell. Now the question is, Who shall prevail? God, or the Pharisee? and whose word shall stand? his, the Pharisee's?

Alas! the Pharisee here must needs come down, for God is greater than all. Also, he hath said, that no flesh shall glory in his presence; and that he will have mercy, and not sacrifice. And again, that it is not (or shall be) in him that wills, nor in him that runs, but in God that sheweth mercy. What hope, help, stay, or relief, then is there left for the merit-monger? What twig, or straw, or twined thread, is left to be a stay for his soul? This besom will sweep away his cobweb: the house that this spider doth so lean upon, will now be overturned, and he in it, to hellfire; for nothing less than everlasting damnation is designed by God, and that for this fearful and unbelieving Pharisee: God will prevail against him for ever.

3. But wilt thou yet plead thy righteousness for mercy? Why, in so doing thou takest away from God the power of giving mercy. For if it be thine as wages, it is no longer his to dispose of at pleasure; for that which another man oweth me, is in equity not at his, but at my disposal. Did I say that by this thy plea thou takest away from God the power of giving mercy? I will add, yea, and also of disposing of heaven and life eternal. And then, I pray you, what is left unto God, and what can he call his own? Not mercy, for that by thy good deeds thou hast purchased: not heaven, for that by thy good deeds thou hast purchased: not eternal life, for that by thy good deeds thou hast purchased. Thus, Pharisee (O thou self-righteous man), hast thou set up thyself above grace, mercy, heaven, glory; yea, above even God himself, for the purchaser should in reason be esteemed above the purchase.

Awake, man! What hast thou done? Thou hast blasphemed God; thou has undervalued the glory of his grace; thou hast, what in thee lieth, opposed the glorious design of heaven; thou hast sought to make thy filthy rags to share in thy justification.

Now, all these are mighty sins; these have made thine iniquity infinite. What wilt thou do? Thou hast created to thyself a world of needless miseries. I call them needless, because thou hadst more than enough before. Thou hast set thyself against God in a way of contending, thou standest upon thy points and pantables; thou wilt not bate God an ace of what thy righteousness is worth, and wilt also make it worth what thyself shalt list: thou wilt be thine own judge, as to the worth of thy righteousness; thou wilt neither hear what verdict the word has passed about it, nor wilt thou endure that God should throw it out in the matter of thy justification, but quarrelest with the doctrine of free grace, or else dost wrest it out of its place to serve thy Pharisaical designs; saying, "God I thank thee, I am not as other men;" fathering upon thyself, yea, upon God and thyself a stark lie; for thou art as other men are, though not in this, yet in that; yea, in a far worse condition than the most of men are. Nor will it help thee anything to attribute this thy goodness to the God of heaven; for that is but a mere toying; the truth is, the God that thou intendest is nothing but thy righteousness; and the grace that thou supposest is nothing but thine own good and honest intentions. So that,

4. In all that thou sayst thou dost but play the downright hypocrite: thou pretendest indeed to mercy, but thou intendest nothing but merit: thou seemest to give the glory to God, but at the same time takest it all to thyself: thou despisest others, and criest up thyself; and in conclusion, fatherest all upon God by word, and upon thyself in truth. Nor is there anything more common among this sort of men, than to make God, his grace, and kindness, the stalking-horse to their own praise, saying, "God, I thank thee," when they trust to themselves that they are righteous, and have not need of any repentance; when the truth is, they are the worst sort of men in the world, because they put themselves into such a state as God hath not put them into, and then impute it to God, saying, God, I thank thee, that thou hast done it; for what greater sin than to make God a liar, or than to father that upon God which he never meant, intended, or did: and all this under colour to glorify God, when there is nothing else designed, but to take all glory from him, and to wear it on thine own head as a crown, and a diadem, in the face of the whole world.

A self-righteous man, therefore, can come to God for mercy no otherwise than fawningly: for what need of mercy hath a righteous man? Let him then talk of mercy, of grace, and goodness, and come in an hundred times with his, "God, I thank thee," in his mouth, all is but words; there is no sense, nor savour, nor relish, of mercy and favour; nor doth he in truth, from his very heart, understand the nature of mercy, nor what is an object thereof; but when he thanks God, he praises himself: when he pleads for mercy, he means his own merit; and all this is manifest from what doth follow; for, saith he, I am not as this Publican: thence clearly insinuating, that not the good, but the bad, should be rejected of the God of heaven: that not the bad but the good, not the sinner, but the self-righteous, are the most proper objects of God's favour. The same thing is done by others in this our day: favour, mercy, grace, and, "God, I thank thee," is in their mouths, but their own strength, sufficiency, free- will, and the like, they are the things they mean by all such high and glorious expressions.

But, secondly, If thy plea be not for mercy, but for justice, then to speak a little to that. 1. Justice has measures and rules to go by; unto which measures and rules, if thou comest not up, justice can do thee no good. Come then, O thou blind Pharisee, let us pass away a few minutes in some discourse about this. Thou demandest justice, because God hath said, that the man that doth these things shall live in and by them. And again, the doers of the law shall be justified, not in a way of mercy, but in a way of justice: "He shall live by them." But what hast thou done, O blind Pharisee? What hast thou done, that thou art emboldened to venture to stand and fall to the most perfect justice of God? Hast thou fulfilled the whole law, and not offended in one point? Hast thou purged thyself from the pollutions and motions of sin that dwell in thy flesh, and work in thy own members? Is the very being of sin rooted out of thy tabernacle? And art thou now as perfectly innocent as ever was Jesus Christ? hast thou, by suffering the uttermost punishment that justice could justly lay upon thee for thy sins, made fair and full satisfaction to God, according to the tenor of his law, for thy transgressions? If thou hast done all these things, then thou mayst plead something, and yet but something, for thyself, in a way of justice. Nay, in this I will assert nothing, but will rather inquire: What hast thou gained by all this thy righteousness? (We will now suppose what must not be granted:) Was not this thy state when thou wast in thy first parents? Wast thou not innocent, perfectly innocent and righteous? And if thou shouldst be so now, what hast thou gained thereby? Suppose that the man that had, forty years ago, forty pounds of his own, and had spent it all since, should yet be able now to shew his forty pounds again; what has he got thereby, or how much richer is he at last than he was when he first set up for himself? Nay, doth not the blot of his ill living betwixt his first and his last, lie as a blemish upon him, unless he should redeem himself also, by works of supererogation, from the scandal that justice may lay at his door for that.

But, I say, suppose, O Pharisee, this should be thy case, yet God is not bound to give thee in justice that eternal which by his grace he bestoweth upon those that have redemption from sin, by the blood of his Son. Injustice, therefore, when all comes to all, thou canst require no more than an endless life in an earthly paradise; for there thou wast set up at first; nor doth it appear from what hath been said, touching all that thou hast done or canst do, that thou deservest a better place.

Did I say, that thou mayst require justly an endless life in an earthly paradise? Why, I must add to that saying this proviso, If thou continuest in the law, and in the righteousness thereof; else not.

But how dost thou know that thou shalt continue therein? Thou hast no promise from God's mouth for that; nor is grace or strength ministered to mankind by the covenant that thou art under. So that still thou standest bound to thy good behaviour; and in the day that thou dost give the first, though ever so little a trip, or stumble in thy obedience, thou forfeitest thine interest in paradise (and in justice), as to any benefit there.

But alas! what need is there that we should thus talk things, when it is manifest that thou hast sinned, not before thou wast a Pharisee, but when after the most strictest sect of thy religion thou livest also a Pharisee; yea, and now in the temple, in thy prayer there, thou shewest thyself to be full of ignorance, pride, self-conceit, and horrible arrogancy, and desire of vain glory, &c., which are none of them the seat or fruits of righteousness, but the seat of the devil, and the fruit of his dwelling, even at this time in thy heart.

Could it ever have been imagined, that such audacious impudence could have put itself forth in any mortal man, in his approach unto God by prayer, as has shewed itself in thee? "I am not as other men," sayst thou! But is this the way to go to God in prayer? "The prayer of the upright is God's delight." But the upright man glorifies God's justice, by confessing to God the vileness and pollution of his state and condition: he glorifies God's mercy, by acknowledging, that that, and that only, as communicated of God by Christ to sinners, can save and deliver from the curse of the law.

This, I say, is the sum of the prayer of the just and upright man, Job. i. 8; xl. 4; Acts xiii. 22; Psalm xxxviii.; li.; 2 Sam. vi. 21, 22; and not as thou most vain-gloriously vauntest with thy, "God, I thank thee, I am not as other men are."

True, when a man is accused by his neighbours, by a brother, by an enemy, and the like, if he be clear (and he may be so, as to what they shall lay to his charge), then let him vindicate, justify, and acquit himself, to the utmost that in justice and truth he can; for his name, the preservation whereof is more to be chosen than silver and gold; also his profession, yea, the name of God too, and religion may now lie at stake, by reason of such false accusations, and perhaps can by no means (as to this man) be covered and vindicated from reproach and scandal, but by his justifying of himself. Wherefore, in such a work, a man serveth God, and saves religion from hurt; yea, as he that is a professor, and has his profession attended with a scandalous life, hurteth religion thereby, so he that has his profession attended with a good life, and shall suffer it notwithstanding to lie under blame by false accusations, when it is in the power of his hand to justify himself, hurteth religion also. But the case of the Pharisee is otherwise. He is not here a-dealing with men, but God; not seeking to stand clear in the sight of the world, but in the sight of heaven itself; and that too, not with respect to what men or angels, but with respect to what God and his law could charge him with, and justly lay at his door.

This therefore mainly altereth the case; for a man here to stand thus upon his point, it is death; for he affronteth God, he giveth him the lie, he reproveth the law; and, in sum, accuseth it of bearing false witness against him; he doth this, I say, even by saying, "God, I thank thee, I am not as other men are;" for God hath made none of this difference. The law condemneth all man as sinners; testifieth that every imagination of the thought of the heart of the sons of men is only evil, and that continually; wherefore they that do as the Pharisee did, to wit, seek to justify themselves before God from the curse of the law by their own good doings, though they also, as the Pharisee did, seem to give God the thanks for all; yet do most horribly sin, even by their so doing, and shall receive a Pharisee's reward at last. Wherefore, O thou Pharisee, it is a vain thing for thee either to think of, or to ask for, at God's hand, either mercy or justice. Because mercy thou canst not ask for, from sense of want of mercy, because thy righteousness, which is by the law, hath utterly blinded thine eyes; and complimenting with God doth nothing: and as for justice, that can do thee no good; but the more just God is, and the more by that he acteth towards thee, the more miserable and fearful will be thy condition, because of the deficiency of thy so much, by thee, esteemed righteousness.

What a deplorable condition then is a poor Pharisee in! For mercy he cannot pray; he cannot pray for it with all his heart, for he seeth indeed no need thereof. True, the Pharisee, though he was impudent enough, yet would not take all from

God; he would still count, that there was due to him a tribute of thanks: "God, I thank thee," saith he: but yet not a bit of this for mercy; but for that he had let him live (for I know not for what he did thank himself), till he had made himself better than other men. But that betterment was a betterment in none other's judgment than that of his own; and that was none other but such an one as was false. So then the Pharisee is by this time quite out of doors: his righteousness is worth nothing, his prayer is worth nothing, his thanks to God are worth nothing; for that what he had was scanty and imperfect, and it was his pride that made him offer it to God for acceptance; nor could his fawning thanksgiving better his case, or make his matter at all good before God.

But I will warrant you, the Pharisee was so far off from thinking thus of himself, and of his righteousness, that he thought of nothing so much as of this, that he was a happy man: yea, happier by far than other his fellow rationals: yea, he plainly declares it, when he saith, "God, I thank thee, I am not as other men are."

O what a fool's paradise was the heart of the Pharisee now in, while he stood in the temple praying to God! God, I thank thee, said he; for I am good and holy; I am a righteous man; I have been full of good works; I am no extortioner, unjust, nor adulterer, nor yet as this wretched Publican. I have kept myself strictly to the rule of mine order, and my order is the most strict of all orders now in being: I fast, I pray, I give tithes of all that I possess. Yea, so forward am I to be a religious man, so ready have I been to listen after my duty, that I have asked both of God and man the ordinances of judgment and justice; I take delight in approaching to God. What less now can be mine than the heavenly kingdom and glory?

Now the Pharisee, like Haman, saith in his heart, To whom would the king delight to do honour more than to myself? Where is the man that so pleaseth God, and, consequently, that in equity and reason should be beloved of God like me? Thus like the prodigal's brother, he pleadeth, saying, "Lo, these many years do I serve thee; neither transgressed I at any time thy commandments," Luke xv. 29. O brave Pharisee! but go on in thine oration--"Nor yet as this Publican."

Poor wretch, quoth the Pharisee to the Publican, What comest thou for? Dost think that such a sinner as thou art shall be heard of God? God heareth not sinners; but if any man be a worshipper of God (as I am, as I thank God I am), him he heareth. Thou, for thy part, hast been a rebel all thy days: I abhor to come nigh thee, or to touch thy garments. Stand by thyself, come not near me, for I am more holy than thou; Isa. lxv. 5.

Hold, stop there, go no further: fie, Pharisee, fie! dost thou know before whom thou standest, to whom thou speakest, and of what the matter of thy silly oration is made? Thou art now before God, thou speakest now to God, and therefore in justice and honesty thou shouldst make mention of his righteousness, not of thine; of his righteousness, and of his only.

I am sure Abraham, of whom thou sayst he is thy father, never had the face to do as thou hast done, though, it is to be presumed, he had more cause so to do than thou hast, or canst have. Abraham had whereof to glory, but not before God; yea, he was called God's friend, and yet would not glory before him; but humbleth himself, was afraid, and trembled in himself, when he stood before him acknowledging of himself to be but dust and ashes; Gen. xviii. 27, 30, 22; Rom. iv. 1, 2; but thou, as thou hadst quite forgot that thou wast framed of that matter, and after the manner of other men, standest and pleadest thy goodness before him? Be ashamed, Pharisee! dost thou think that God hath eyes of flesh, or that he seeth as man sees? Are not the secrets of thy heart open unto him Thinkest thou with thyself that thou, with a few of thy defiled ways, canst cover thy rotten wall, that thou has daubed with untempered mortar, and so hide the dirt thereof from his eyes; or that these fine, smooth, and oily words, that come out of thy mouth, will make him forget that thy throat is an open sepulchre, and that thou within art full of dead men's bones, and all uncleanness? Thy thus cleansing of the outside of the cup and platter, and thy garnishing of the sepulchres of the righteous, is nothing at all in God's eyes, but things that manifest that thou art an hypocrite and blind, because thou takest no notice of that which is within, which yet is that which is most abominable to God. For the fruit, alas! what is the fruit of the tree, or what are the streams of the fountain? Thy fountain is defiled; yea, a defiler, and so that which maketh the whole self, with thy works, unclean in God's sight.

But, Pharisee, how comes it to pass that the poor Publican is now so much a mote in thine eye, that thou canst not forbear, but must accuse him before the judgment-seat of God--for in that thou sayst, that thou art not even as this Publican, thou bringest in an accusation, a charge, a bill, against him? What has he done? Has he concealed any of thy righteousness? or has he secretly informed against thee, that thou art an hypocrite and superstitious? I dare say, the poor wretch has neither meddled nor made with thee in these matters.

But what aileth thee, Pharisee? Doth the poor Publican stand to vex thee? Doth he touch thee with his dirty garments? or doth he annoy thee with his stinking breath? Doth his posture of standing so like a man condemned offend thee? True, he now standeth with his hand held up at God's bar; he pleads guilty to all that is laid to his charge.

He cannot strut, vapour, and swagger as thou dost; but why offended at this? Oh, but he has been a naughty man, and I have been righteous! sayst thou. Well, Pharisee, well, his naughtiness shall not be laid to thy charge, if thou hast chosen none of his ways. But since thou wilt yet bear me down that thou art righteous, shew now, even now, while thou standest before God with the Publican, some, though they be but small, yea, though but very small, fruits of thy righteousness. Let the Publican alone, since he is speaking for his life before God. Or, if thou canst not let him alone, yet do not speak against him; for thy so doing will but prove that thou rememberest the evil that the man has done unto thee; yea, and that thou bearest him a grudge for it too, and while you stand before God.

But, Pharisee, the righteous man is a merciful man, and while he standeth praying, he forgiveth; yea, and also crieth to God that he will forgive him too; Mark xi. 25, 26; Acts vii. 60. Hitherto then thou hast shewed none of the fruits of thy righteousness. Pharisee, righteousness would teach thee to love this Publican, but thou shewest that thou hatest him. Love covereth the multitude of sins; but hatred and unfaithfulness revealeth secrets.

Pharisee, thou shouldst have remembered this thy brother in this his day of adversity, and shouldst have shewed that thou hadst compassion on thy brother in this his deplorable condition; but thou, like the proud, the cruel, and the arrogant man, hast taken thy neighbour at the advantage, and that when he is even between the straits, and standing upon the pinnacle of difficulty, betwixt the heavens and the hells, and hast done what thou couldst, what on thy part lay, to thrust him down to the deep, saying, "I am not even as this Publican."

What cruelty can be greater, what rage more furious, and what spite and hatred more damnable and implacable, than to follow, or take a man while he is asking of mercy at God's hands, and to put in a caveat against his obtaining of it, by exclaiming against him that he is a sinner? The master of righteousness doth not so: "Do not think (saith he) that I will accuse you to the Father." The scholars of righteousness do not do so. "But as for me (said David), when they (mine enemies) were sick (and the Publican here was sick of the most malignant disease), my clothing was of sackcloth, I humbled my soul with fasting, and my prayer (to wit, that I made for them) returned into mine own bosom. I behaved myself as though he had been my friend or brother: I bowed down heavily, as one that mourneth for his mother;" John v. 45; Psalm xxxv. 13, 14.

Pharisee, dost thou see here how contrary thou art to righteous men? Now then, where shall we find out one to parallel thee, but by finding him out that is called "the dragon;" for he it is that accuseth the poor sinners before God? Zech. iii.; Rev. xii.

"I am not as this Publican." Modesty should have commanded thee to have bit thy tongue as to this. What could the angels think, but that revenge was now in thine heart, and but that thou comest up into the temple rather to boast of thyself and accuse thy neighbour, than to pray to the God of heaven; for what petition is there in all thy prayer, that gives the least intimation that thou hast the knowledge of God or thyself? Nay, what petition of any kind is there in thy vain-glorious oration from first to last? Only an accusation drawn up, and that against one helpless and forlorn; against a poor man, because he is a sinner; drawn up, I say, against him by thee, who canst not make proof of thyself that thou art righteous; but come to proofs of righteousness, and thou art wanting also. What, though thy raiment is better than his, thy skin may be full as black; yea, what if thy skin be whiter than his, thy heart may be yet far blacker. Yea, it is so, for the truth hath spoken it; for within, you are full of excess and all uncleanness; Matt. xxiii.

Pharisee, these are transgressions against the second table, and the Publican shall be guilty of them; but there are sins also against the first table, and thou thyself art guilty of them.

The Publican, in that he was an extortioner, unjust and an adulterer, made it thereby manifest that he did not love his neighbour; and thou by making a god, a saviour, a deliverer, of thy filthy righteousness, dost make it appear, that thou dost not love thy God; for as he that taketh, or that derogateth from his neighbour in that which is his neighbour's due, sinneth against his neighbour; so he that taketh or derogateth from God, sinneth against God.

Now, then, though thou hast not, as thou dost imagine, played at that low game as to derogate from thy neighbour; yet thou hast played at that high game as to derogate from thy God; for thou hast robbed God of the glory of salvation; yea, declared, that as to that there is no trust to be put in him. "Lo, this is the man that made not God his strength; but trusted in the abundance of his riches, and strengthened himself in his wickedness;" Psalm lii. 7.

What else means this great bundle of thy own righteousness, which thou hast brought with thee into the temple? yea, what means else thy commending of thyself because of that, and so thy implicit prayer, that thou for that mightst find acceptance with God?

All this, what does it argue, I say, but thy diffidence of God? and that thou countest salvation safer in thine own righteousness than in the righteousness of God? and that thy own love to, and care of thy own soul, is far greater, and so much better, than is the care and love of God? And is this to keep the first table; yea, the first branch of that table, which saith, "Thou shalt love the Lord thy God?" for thy thus doing cannot stand with love to God?

How can that man say, I love God, who from his very heart shrinketh to trust in him? Or, how can that man say, I would glorify God, who in his very heart refuseth to stand and fall by his mercy?

Suppose a great man should bid all the poor of the parish to his house to dinner, and should moreover send by the mouth of his servant, saying, My lord hath killed his fatlings, hath furnished his table, and prepared his wine, nor is there want of anything; come to the banquet: Would it not be counted as an high affront to, great contempt of, and much distrust in, the goodness of the man of the house, if some of these guests should take with them, out of their own poor store, some of their mouldy crusts, and carry them with them, lay them on their trenchers upon the table before the lord of the feast and the rest of his guests, out of fear that he yet would not provide sufficiently for those he had bidden to the dinner that he had made?

Why, Pharisee, this is the very case; thou hast been called to a banquet, even to the banquet of God's grace, and thou hast been disposed to go; but behold, thou hast not believed that he would of his own cost make thee a feast when thou comest:

wherefore of thy own store thou hast brought with thee, and hast laid upon thy trencher on his table thy mouldy crusts in the presence of the angels, and of this poor Publican; yea, and hast vauntingly said upon the whole, "God, I thank thee, I am not as other men are." I am no such needy man; Luke xviii. 11. "I am no extortioner, nor unjust, nor adulterer, nor even as this Publican." I am come indeed to thy feast, for of civility I could do no less; but for thy dainties, I need them not, I have of such things enough of mine own; Luke xviii. 12. I thank thee therefore for thy offer of kindness, but I am not as those that have, and stand in need thereof, "nor yet as this Publican." And thus feeding upon thine own fare, or by making a composition of his and thine together, thou contemnest God, thou countest him insufficient or unfaithful; that is, either one that has not enough, or having it, will not bestow it upon the poor and needy; and, therefore, of mere pretence thou goest to his banquet, but yet trustest to thy own, and to that only.

This is to break the first table; and so to make thyself a sinner of the highest form: for the sins against the first table are sins of an higher nature than are the sins against the second. True, the sins of the second table are also sins against God, because they are sins against the commandments of God: but the sins that are against the first table, are sins not only against the command, but against the very love, strength, holiness, and faithfulness of God: and herein stands thy condition; thou hast not, thou sayst, thou hast not done injury to thy neighbour; but what of that, if thou hast reproached thy maker?

Pharisee, I will assure thee, thou art beside the saddle; thy state is not good, thy righteousness is so far off from doing any good, that it maketh thee to be a greater sinner, because it signifieth more immediately against the mercy, the love, the grace, and goodness of God, than the sins of other sinners, as to degree, do.

And as they are more odious and abominable in the sight of God (as they needs must, if what is said be true, as it is), so they are more dangerous to the life and soul of man; for that they always appear unto him in whom they dwell, and to him that trusteth in them, not to be sins and transgressions, but virtues and excellent things; not things that set a man further off, but the things that bring a man nearer God, than those that want them are or can be.

This therefore is the dangerous estate of those that go about to establish their own righteousness, that neither have, nor can, while they are so doing, submit themselves to the righteousness of God; Rom. x. 3. It is far more easy to persuade a poor wretch, whose life is debauched, and sins are written in his forehead, to submit to the righteousness of God (that is, to the righteousness that is of God's providing and giving), than it is to persuade a self-righteous man to do it; for the profane is sooner convinced of the necessity of righteousness to save him, as that he has none of his own, and accepteth of, and submitteth himself to the help and salvation that is in the righteousness and obedience of another.

And upon this account it is that Christ saith the publicans and harlots enter into the kingdom of heaven before the scribes and Pharisees; Matt. xxi. 31. Poor Pharisee, what a loss art thou at? thou art not only a sinner, but a sinner of the highest form. Not a sinner by such sins (by such sins chiefly) as the second table doth make manifest; but a sinner chiefly in that way as no self-righteous man did ever dream of. For when the righteous man or Pharisee shall hear that he is a sinner, he replieth, "I am not as other men are."

And because the common and more ordinary description of sin is the transgression against the second table, he presently replieth again, "I am not as this Publican is;" and so shroudeth himself under his own lame endeavours and ragged partial patches of moral or civil righteousness. Wherefore, when he heareth that his righteousness is condemned, slighted, and accounted nothing worth, then he fretteth and fumeth, and would kill the man that so slighteth and disdaineth his goodly righteousness; but Christ, and the true gospel-teacher still go on, and condemn all his righteousness as menstruous rags, as an abomination to God, and nothing but loss and dung.

Now menstruous rags, things that are an abomination and dung, are not fit matter to make a garment of to wear when I come to God for life, much less to be made my friend, my advocate, my mediator and spokesman, when I stand betwixt heaven and hell; Isa. lxiv. 6; Luke xvi. 15; Phil. iii. 6-8, to plead for me that I might be saved.

Perhaps some will blame me, and count me also worthy thereof, because I do not distinguish betwixt the matter and the manner of the Pharisee's righteousness. And let them condemn me still for saving the holy law, which is neither the matter nor manner of the Pharisee's righteousness, but rather the rules (if he will live thereby) up to which he should completely come in every thing that he doth. And

I say again, that the whole of the Pharisee's righteousness is sinful, though not with and to men, yet with and before the God of heaven. Sinful, I say it is, and abominable, both in itself, and also in its effects.

1. In itself; for that it is imperfect, scanty, and short of the rule by which righteousness is enjoined, and even with which every act should be; for shortness here, even every shortness in these duties, is sin and sinful weakness; wherefore the curse taketh hold of the man for coming short; but that it could not justly do, if his coming short was not his sin: Cursed is every one that doth not, and that continueth not to do all things written in the law; Deut. xxvii. 26; Gal. iii. 10.

2. It is sinful; because it is wrought by sinful flesh; for all legal righteousness is a work of the flesh; Rom. iv. 1, &c.; Phil. iii. 3-8.

A work, I say, of the flesh; even of that flesh, who, or which also committeth the greatest enormities; for the flesh is but one, though its workings are divers: sometimes in a way most notoriously sensual and devilish, causing the soul to wallow in the mire.

But these are not all the works of the flesh; the flesh sometimes will attempt to be righteous, and set upon doing actions that in their perfection would be very glorious and beautiful to behold. But because the law is only commanding words, and yieldeth no help to the man that attempts to perform it; and because the flesh is weak, and cannot do of itself that, therefore this most glorious work of the flesh faileth.

But, I say, as it is a work of the flesh it cannot be good, forasmuch as the hand that worketh it is defiled with sin; for in a good man, one spiritually good, that is "in his flesh, there dwells no good thing," but consequently that which is bad; how then can the flesh of a carnal, graceless man (and such a one is every Pharisee and self- righteous man in the world), produce, though it joineth itself to the law, to the righteous law of God, that which is good in his sight.

If any shall think that I pinch too hard, because I call man's righteousness which is of the law, of the righteous law of God, flesh, let them consider that which follows: to wit, That though man by sin is said "to be dead in sin and trespasses," yet not so dead but that he can act still in his own sphere; that is, to do, and choose to do, either that which by all men is counted base, or that which by some is counted good, though he is not, nor can all the world make him, capable of doing any thing that may please his God.

Man, by nature, as dead as he is, can, and that with the will of his flesh, will his own salvation. Man, by nature, can, and that by the power of the flesh, pursue and follow after his own salvation; but then he wills it, and pursues or follows after it, not in God's way, but his own; not by faith in Christ, but by the law of Moses. See Rom. ix. 16, 31; x. 3, 7.

Wherefore it is no error to say, that a man naturally has will, and a power to pursue his will, and that as to his own salvation. But it is a damnable error to say, that he hath will and power to pursue it, and that in God's way: for then we must hold that the mysteries of the gospel are natural; for that natural men, or men by nature, may apprehend and know them, yea, and know them to be the only means by which they must obtain eternal life; for the understanding must act before the will; yea, a man must approve of the way to life by Jesus Christ, before his mind will budge, or stir, or move, that way: "But the natural man receiveth not the things of the Spirit of God (of the gospel); for they are foolishness to him; neither can he know them, because they are spiritually discerned."

He receiveth not these things; that is, his mind and will lie cross unto them, for he counts them foolishness; nor can all the natural wisdom in the world cause that his will should fall in with them, because it cannot discern them.

Nature discerneth the law, and the righteousness thereof; yea, it discerneth it, and approveth thereof; that is, that the righteousness of it is the best and only way to life, and therefore the natural will and power of the flesh, as here you see in the Pharisee, do steer their course by that to eternal life; 1 Cor. ii. 14.

The righteousness of the law, therefore, is a work of the flesh, a work of sinful flesh, and therefore must needs be as filth, and dung, and abominable as to that for which this man hath produced it and presented it in the temple before God.

Nor is the Pharisee alone entangled in this mischief; many souls are by these works of the flesh flattered, as also the Pharisee was, into an opinion, that their state is good, when there is nothing in it. The most that their conversion amounteth to is, the Publican is become a Pharisee; the open sinner is become a self-righteous man. Of the black side of the flesh he hath had enough, now therefore with the white side of the flesh he will recreate himself. And now, most wicked must he needs be that questioneth the goodness of the state of such a man. He, of a drunkard, a swearer, an unclean person, a Sabbath-breaker, a liar, and the like, is become re-formed, a lover of righteousness, a strict observer, doer, and trader in the formalities of the law, and a herder with men of his complexion. And now he is become a great exclaimer against sin and sinners, denying to be acquaint with those that once were his companions, saying, "I am not even as this Publican."

To turn therefore from sin to man's righteousness, yea, to rejoice in confidence, that thy state is better than is that of the Publican (I mean, better in the eyes of divine justice, and in the judgment of the law); and yet to be found by the law, not in the spirit, but in the flesh; not in Christ, but under the law; not in a state of sal-vation, but of damnation, is common among men: for they, and they only, are the right men, "who worship God in the spirit, and rejoice in Christ Jesus, and have no confidence in the flesh." Where, by "flesh," must not be meant the horrible trans-gressions against the law (though they are also called "the works of the flesh," Gal. iv. 29); for they minister no occasion unto men to have confidence in them towards God: but that is that which is insinuated by Paul, where he saith, he had no "con-fidence in the flesh," though he might have had it; as he said, "though I might also have confidence in the flesh." "If any other man," saith he, "thinketh that he hath whereof he might trust in the flesh, I more," Phil. iii. 3, 4; and then he repeats a twofold privilege that he had by the flesh.

1. That he was one of the seed of Abraham, and of the tribe of Benjamin, an Hebrew of the Hebrews, &c.

2. That he had fallen in with the strictest men of that religion, which was such after the flesh, to wit, to be a Pharisee, and was the son of a Pharisee, had much fleshly zeal for God, and "touching the righteousness which is of the law, blame-less," Phil. iii. 3, 5, 6.

But I say still, there is nothing but flesh; fleshly privileges and fleshly righ-teousness, and so, consequently, a fleshly confidence, and trust for heaven. This is manifest; when the man had his eyes enlightened, he counted all loss and dung that he might be found in Christ, not having his own righteousness, which is of the law, but that which is through the faith of Christ, the righteousness which is of God by faith.

And this leads me to another thing, and that is, to tell thee, O thou blind Phari-see, that thou canst not be in a safe condition, because thou hast thy confidence in the flesh, that is, in the righteousness of the flesh. "For all flesh is grass, and all the glory of it as the flower of the field;" and the flesh, and the glory of that being as weak as the grass, which to-day is, and to-morrow is cast into the oven, is but a weak business for a man to venture his eternal salvation upon. Wherefore, as I also hinted before, the godly-wise have been afraid to be found in their righteousness, I mean their own personal righteousness, though that is far better than can be the righteousness of any carnal man: for the godly man's righteousness is wrought by the Spirit and faith of Christ, but the ungodly man's righteousness is of the flesh, and of the law. Yet I say, this godly man is afraid to stand by his righteousness before the tribunal of God, as is manifest in these following particulars.

1. He sees sin in his righteousness; for so the prophet intimates, when he saith, "All our righteousnesses are as filthy rags" (Isa. lxiv.); but there is nothing can make one's righteousness filthy but sin. It is not the poor, the low, the mean, the sickly, the beggarly state of man, nor yet his being hated of devils, persecuted of men, broken under necessities, reproaches, distresses, or any kind of troubles of this nature that can make the godly man's righteousness filthy; nothing but sin can do it, and that can, doth, hath, and will do it. Nor can any man, be he who he will, and though he watches, prays, strives, denies himself, and puts his body under what chastisement or hardships he can; yea, though he also get his spirit and soul hoisted up to the highest peg or pin of sanctity and holy contemplation, and so his lusts to the greatest degree of mortification; but sin will be with him in the best of his performances: with him, I say, to pollute and defile his duties, and to make his righteousness speckled and spotted, filthy and menstruous.

I will give you two or three instances for this.

(1.) Nehemiah was a man (in his day), one that was zealous, very zealous, for God, for his house, for his people, and for his ways; and so continued, and that from first to last, as they may see that please to read the relation of his actions; yet when he comes seriously to be concerned with God about his duties, he relinquisheth a standing by them. True, he mentioneth them to God, but confesseth that there are imperfections in them, and prayeth that God will not wipe them away. "Wipe not out my good deeds, O my God, that I have done for the house of my God, and for the offices thereof." And again, "Remember me, O my God, concerning this also (another good deed), and spare me according to the greatness of thy mercy; and remember me, O my God, for good;" Neh. xiii.

I do not think that by these prayers he pleadeth for an acceptance of his person, as touching justification from the curse of the law (as the poor blind Pharisee doth), but that God would accept of his service, as he was a son, and not deny to give him a reward of grace for what he had done, since he was pleased to declare in his testament, that he would reward the labour of love of his saints with an exceeding weight of glory; and therefore prayeth, that God would not wipe away his good deeds, but remember him for good, according to the greatness of his mercy.

(2.) A second instance is that of David, where he saith, "Enter not into judgment with thy servant, O Lord; for in thy sight shall no man living be justified;" Psalm clxiii. 2. David, as I have hinted before, is said to be a man "after God's own heart," Acts xiii.; and as here by the Spirit he acknowledges him for his servant; yet behold how he shrinketh, how he draweth back, how he prayeth, and petitioneth, that God would vouchsafe so much as not to enter into judgment with him. Lord, saith he, if thou enterest into judgment with me, I die, because I shall be condemned; for in thy sight I cannot be justified; to wit, by my own good deeds. Lord, at the beginning of thy dealing with me, by the law and my works, I die: therefore do not so much as enter into judgment with me, O Lord. Nor is this my case only, but it is the condition of all the world: "For in thy sight shall no man living be justified."

(3.) A third instance is that general conclusion of the apostle, "But that no man is justified by the law in the sight of God is evident; for the just shall live by faith." By this saying of St Paul, as he taketh up the sentence of the prophet Habakkuk, chap. ii. 4, so he taketh up this sentence, yea, and the personal justice of David also. No man, saith he, is justified by the law in the sight of God: no, no just man, no holy man, not the strictest and most righteous man. But why not? Why, because "the just shall live by faith."

The just man, therefore, must die, if he has not faith in another righteousness than that which is of the law, called his own: I say, he must die, if he has none other righteousness than that which is his own by the law. Thus also Paul confesses of himself: "I (saith he) know nothing by myself," either before conversion or after; that is, I knew not that I did any thing before conversion, either against the law, or against my conscience; for I was then, touching the righteousness which is of the law, blameless. Also, since my conversion, I know nothing by myself; for "I have walked in all good conscience before God unto this day."

A great saying, I promise you. Well, but yet "I am not hereby justified;" Phil. iii. 7; Acts xxiii. 1; 1 Cor. iv. 4. Nor will I dare to venture the eternal salvation of my soul upon mine own justice; "for he that judgeth me is the Lord;" that is, though I, through my dim-sightedness, cannot see the imperfections of my righteousness, yet the Lord, who is my judge, and before whose tribunal I must shortly stand, can and will; and if in his sight there shall be found no more but one spot in my righteousness, I must, if I plead my righteousness, fall for that.

2. That the best of men are afraid to stand before God's tribunal, there to be judged by the law as to life and death, according to the sufficiency or non-sufficiency of their righteousness, is evident; because by casting away their own (in this matter), they make all the means they can for this; that is, that his mercy, by an act of grace, be made over to them, and that they in it may stand before God to be judged.

Hence David cries out so often, "Lead me in thy righteousness." "Deliver me in thy righteousness." "Judge me according to thy righteousness." "Quicken me in thy righteousness." "O Lord (says he), give ear to my supplications: in thy faithfulness answer me, and in thy righteousness." "And enter not into judgment with thy servant, O Lord: for in thy sight shall no flesh living be justified." And David, what if God doth thus? Why, then, saith he, "My tongue shall speak of his righteousness." "My tongue shall sing of thy righteousness." "My mouth shall shew forth thy righteousness." "Yea, I will make mention of thy righteousness, even of thine only;" Psalm lviii.; xxxi. 1; xxxv. 24; cxix. 40; xxxv. 28; li. 14; lxxi. 15, 16.

Daniel also, when he comes to plead for himself and his people, he first casts away his and their righteousness, saying, "For we do not present our supplications unto thee for our righteousness:" And he pleads God's righteousness, and that he might have a share and interest in that saying, "O Lord, righteousness belongeth to thee;" to wit, that righteousness, for the sake of which, mercy and forgiveness, and so heaven and happiness, is extended to us.

Righteousness belongeth to thee, and is thine, as nearly as sin, shame, and confusion, are ours, and belongeth to us. Read the 16th and 17th verses of the 9th of Daniel. "O Lord (saith he), according to all thy righteousness, I beseech thee, let thine anger, and thy fury, be turned away from thy city Jerusalem, thy holy mountain; because for our sins, and for the iniquities of our fathers, Jerusalem, and thy people, are become a reproach to all that are about us. Now, therefore, O our God, hear the prayer of thy servant, and his supplications, and cause thy face to shine upon thy sanctuary that is desolate, for the Lord's sake:" For the sake of the Lord Jesus Christ; for on him Daniel now had his eye, and through him to the Father he made his supplication; yea, and the answer was according to his prayer, to wit, that God would have mercy on Jerusalem; and that he would in his time send the Lord, the Messias, to bring them in everlasting righteousness for them.

Paul also, as I have hinted before, disclaims his own righteousness, and layeth fast hold on the righteousness of God; seeking to be found in that, not having his own righteousness, for he knew that when the rain descends, the winds blow, and the floods come down on all men, they that have but their own righteousness, must fall; Phil. iii

Now, the earnest desire of the righteous to be found in God's righteousness, ariseth from strong conviction of the imperfections of their own, and the knowledge that was given them of the terror that will attend men at the day of the fiery trial; to wit, the day of judgement. For although men can now flatter themselves into a fool's paradise, and persuade themselves that all shall be well with them then, for the sake of their own silly and vain-glorious performances, yet when the day comes that shall burn like an oven, and when all that have done wickedly shall be as stubble (and so will all appear to be that are not found in Christ), then will their righteousness vanish like smoke, or be like fuel for that burning flame. And hence the righteousness that the godly seek to be found in, is called, The name of the Lord, a strong tower, a rock, a shield, a fortress, a buckler, a rock of defence, unto which they resort, and into which they run and are safe.

The godly therefore do not, as this Pharisee, bring their own righteousness into the temple, and there buoy up themselves and spirits by that into a conceit, that for the sake of that God will be merciful and good unto them; but throwing away their own, they make to God for his, because they certainly know, even by the word of God, that in the judgment none can stand the trial but those that are found in the righteousness of God.

3. That the best of men are afraid to stand before God's tribunal by the law, there to be judged to life and death, according to the sufficiency or non-sufficiency

of their righteousness, is evident; for they know, that it is a vain thing to seek, by acts of righteousness, to make themselves righteous men, as is the way of all them that seek to be justified by the deeds of the law.

And herein lieth the great difference between the Pharisee and the true Christian man. The Pharisee thinks, by acts of righteousness, he shall make himself a righteous man: therefore he cometh into the presence of God well furnished, as he thinks, with his negative and positive righteousness.

Grace suffereth not a man to boast before God, whatever he saith before men. His soul that is lifted up, is not upright in him; and better is the poor in spirit than the proud in spirit. The Pharisee was a very proud man; a proud, ignorant man; proud of his own righteousness, and ignorant of God's: for had he not, he could not, as he did, have so condemned the Publican, and justified himself.

And I say again, that all this pride and vain-glorious show of the Pharisee did arise from his not being acquainted with this, that a man must be good before he can do good; he must be righteous, before he can do righteousness. This is evident from Paul, who insinuateth this as the reason why none do good, even because "There is none that is righteous, no, not one." "There is none righteous," saith he, and then follows, "There is none that doeth good;" Rom. iii. 10, 11, 12. For it is not possible for a man that is not first made righteous by the God of heaven, to do any thing that in a gospel-sense may be called righteousness. To make himself a righteous man, by his so meddling with them, he may design; but work righteousness, and so by such works of righteousness make himself a righteous man, he cannot.

The righteousness of a carnal man is indeed by God called righteousness; but it must be understood as spoken in the dialect of the world. The world indeed calls it righteousness, and it will do no harm, if it bear that term with reference to worldly matters. Hence worldly civilians are called good and righteous men, and so, such as Christ, under that notion, neither died for, nor giveth his grace unto; Rom. v. 7, 8. But we are not now discoursing about any other righteousness, than that which is so accounted either in a law or in a gospel-sense; and therefore let us a little more touch upon that.

A man then must be righteous in a law-sense, before he can do acts of righteousness, I mean, that are such in a gospel-sense. Hence, first, you have true gospel-righteousness made the fruit of a second birth. "If ye know that Christ is righteous, know ye that every one that doeth righteousness is born of him;" 1 John ii. 29. Not born of him by virtue of his own righteous actions, but born of him by virtue of Christ's mighty working with his work upon the soul, who afterwards, from a principle of life, acteth and worketh righteousness.

And he saith again, "Little children, let no man deceive you: he that doeth righteousness is righteous, even as he is righteous." Upon this scripture I will a little comment, for the proof of what is urged before: namely, that a man must be righteous in a law-sense, before he can do such things that may be called acts of righteousness in a gospel-sense. And for this, this scripture, 1 John iii. 7, ministereth to us two things to be considered by us.

The first is, That he that doth righteousness is righteous.

The second is, That he that doth righteousness is righteous, as Christ is righteous.

First, He that doth righteousness; that is, righteousness which the gospel calleth so, is righteous; that is, precedent to, or before he doth that righteousness. For he doth not say, he shall make his person righteous by acts of righteousness that he shall do; for then an evil tree may bear good fruit, yea, and may make itself good by doing so; but he saith, He that doth righteousness is righteous; as he saith, He that doth righteousness is born of him.

So then, a man must be righteous before he can do righteousness, before he can do righteousness in a gospel-sense.

Our second thing then is to inquire, with what righteousness a man must be righteous, before he can do that which in a gospel-sense is called righteousness.

And, first, I answer, he must be righteous in a law-sense: that is, he must be righteous in the judgment of the law. This is evident: because he saith, "He that doeth righteousness is righteous, as he is righteous." That is, in a law-sense: for Christ in no sense is righteous in the judgment of charity only; but in his meanest acts, if it be lawful to make such comparison, he was righteous in a law- sense, or in the judgment of the law. Now the apostle saith, that "he that doeth righteousness is righteous, as he is righteous." They are the words of God, and therefore I cannot err in quoting of them, though I may not so fully as I would make the glory of them shine in speaking to them.

But what righteousness is that, with which a man must stand righteous in the judgment of the law, before he shall or can be found to do acts of righteousness, that by the gospel are so called?

1. I answer, first, It is none of his own which is of the law, you may be sure: for he hath his righteousness before he doth any that can be called his own. "He that doeth righteousness is righteous" already, precedent to, or before he doth that righteousness; yea, he "is righteous, even as he is righteous."

2. It cannot be his own which is of the gospel; that is, that which floweth from a principle of grace in the soul: for he is righteous before he doth this righteousness. "He that doeth righteousness is righteous." He doth not say, he that hath done it, but he that doth it; respecting the act while it is in doing, he is righteous. He is righteous even then when he is a-doing of the very first act of righteousness; but an act, while it is doing, cannot, until it is done, be called an act of righteousness; yet, saith the text, "he is righteous."

But again, if an act, while it is doing, cannot be called an act of righteousness, to be sure, it cannot have such influences as to make the actor righteous--to make him righteous, as the Son of God is righteous; and yet the righteousness with which this doer is made righteous, and that before he doth righteousness, is such; for so saith the text, that makes him righteous, as he is righteous.

Besides, it cannot be his own, which is gospel-righteousness, flowing from a principle of grace in the soul; for that in its greatest perfection in us, while we live in this world, is accompanied with some imperfections; to wit, our faith, love, and whole course of holiness is wanting, or hath something lacking in it. They neither are apart, nor when put all together, perfect, as to the degree, the uttermost degree of perfection.

But the righteousness under consideration, with which the man, in that of John, is made righteous, is a perfect righteousness; not only with respect to the nature of it, as a penny is as perfect silver as a shilling; nor yet with respect to a comparative degree, for so a shilling arriveth more toward the perfection of the number twenty, than doth a twopenny or a threepenny piece; but it is a righteousness so perfect, that nothing can be added to, nor can any thing be taken from it; for so implieth the words of the text, he is righteous as Christ is righteous; yea, thus righteous before, and in order to his doing of righteousness.

And in this he is like unto the Son of God, who was also righteous before he did acts of righteousness referring to a law of commandment; wherefore it is said, that as he is, so are we in this world. As he is or was righteous, before he did acts of righteousness among men by a law; so are his righteous, before they act righteousness among men by a law. "He that doeth righteousness is righteous, as he is righteous."

Christ was righteous before he did righteousness, with a twofold righteousness. He had a righteousness as he was God; his Godhead was perfectly righteous: yea, it was righteousness itself. His human nature was perfectly righteous, it was naturally spotless and undefiled. Thus his person was righteous, and so qualified to do that righteousness, that because he was born of woman, and made under the law, he was bound by the law to perform.

Now, as he is, so are we; not by way of natural righteousness, but by way of resemblance thereunto. Had Christ, in order to his working of righteousness, a two fold righteousness inherent in himself?--the Christian, in order to his working of righteousness, had belonging to him a twofold righteousness. Did Christ's twofold righteousness qualify him for that work of righteousness that was of God designed for him to do?--why, the Christian's twofold righteousness doth qualify him for that work of righteousness that God hath ordained that he should do and walk in this world.

But you may ask, What is that righteousness with which a Christian is made righteous before he doth righteousness?

I answer, It is a twofold righteousness.

1. It is a righteousness put upon him.

2. It is a righteousness put into him.

For the first, It is a righteousness put upon him, with which also he is clothed as with a coat or mantle, Rom. iii. 22, and this is called "the robe of righteousness;" and this is called "the garment of salvation;" Isa. lxi. 10.

This righteousness is none other but the obedience of Christ; the which he performed in the days of his flesh, and can properly be called no man's righteousness, but the righteousness of Christ; because no man had a hand therein, but he completed it himself. And hence it is said, that "by the obedience of one shall many be made righteous;" Rom. v. 19. By the obedience of one, of one man Jesus Christ (as you have it in verse 15); for he came down into the world, to this very end; that is, to make a generation righteous, not by making of them laws, and prescribing unto them rules (for this was the work of Moses, who said, "And it shall be our righteousness, if we observe to do all these commandments before the Lord our God, as he hath commanded us;" Deut. vi. 25; xxiv. 13); nor yet by taking away by his grace the imperfections of their righteousness, and so making of that perfect by additions of his own; but he makes them righteous by his obedience, not in them, but for them, while he personally subjected himself to his Father's law on our behalf, that he might have a righteousness to bestow upon us. And hence we are said to be made righteous, while we work not, and to be justified, while ungodly (Rom. iv. 5), which can be done by no other righteousness than that which is the righteousness of Christ by performance, the righteousness of God by donation, and our righteousness by imputation. For, I say, the person that wrought this righteousness for us, is Jesus Christ; the person that giveth it to us, is the Father; who hath made Christ to be unto us righteousness, and hath given him to us for this very end, that we might be made the righteousness of God in him; 1 Cor. i. 4; 2 Cor. v. 21. And hence it is often said, "One shall say, Surely in the Lord have I righteousness and strength." And again, "In the Lord shall all the seed of Israel be justified, and shall glory." "This is the heritage of the servants of the Lord; and their righteousness is of me, saith the Lord;" Isa. xlv. 24, 25; liv. 17.

This righteousness is that which justifieth, and which secureth the soul from the curse of the law; by hiding, through its perfection, all the sins and imperfections of the soul. Hence it follows, "Even as David also describeth the blessedness of the man unto whom God imputeth righteousness without works, saying, Blessed are they whose iniquities are forgiven, and whose sins are covered. Blessed is the man to whom the Lord will not impute sin;" Rom. iv.

And this it doth, even while the person, that by grace is made a partaker, is without good works, and so ungodly. This is the righteousness of Christ, Christ's personal performances, which he did when he was in this world; that is that by which the soul, while naked, is covered, and so hid as to its nakedness, from the divine sentence of the law: "I spread my skirt over thee, and covered thy nakedness," Ezek. xvi. 4-9.

Now this obediential righteousness of Christ consisteth of two parts. 1. In a doing of that which the law commanded us to do. 2. In a paying that price for the transgression thereof, which justice hath said shall be required at the hand of man; and that is the cursed death. "In the day that thou eatest thereof, thou shalt surely die the death;" to wit, the death that comes by the curse of the law. So then, Christ having brought in that part of obedience for us, which consisteth in a doing of such obediential acts of righteousness which the law commands, he adds thereto the spilling of his blood, to be the price of our redemption from that cursed death, that by sin we had brought upon our bodies and souls. And thus are the Christians perfectly righteous; they have the whole obedience of Christ made over to them; to wit, that obedience that standeth in doing the law, and that obedience that standeth in paying of a price for our transgressions. So, then, doth the law call for righteousness? here it is. Doth the law call for satisfaction for our sins? Here it is. And what can the law say any more to the sinner but that which is good, when he findeth in the personal obedience of Christ for him, that which answereth to what it can command, that which it can demand of us?

Herein, then, standeth a Christian's safety, not in a bundle of actions of his own, but in a righteousness which cometh to him by grace and gift; for this righteousness is such as comes by gift, by the gift of God. Hence it is called the gift of righteousness, the gift by grace, the gift of righteousness by grace, which is the righteousness of one, to wit, the obedience of Jesus Christ, Rom. v. 15-19.

And this is the righteousness by which he that doth righteousness is righteous as he is righteous; because it is the very self-same righteousness that the Son of God hath accomplished by himself. Nor has he any other or more excellent righteousness, of which the law taketh notice, or that it requireth, than this: for as for the righteousness of his Godhead, the law is not concerned with that; for as he is such, the law is his creature, and servant, and may not meddle with him.

The righteousness also of his human nature, the law hath nothing to do with that; for that is the workmanship of God, and is as good, as pure, as holy, and undefiled, as is the law itself. All then that the law hath to do with, is to exact complete obedience of him that is made under it, and a due satisfaction for the breach thereof; the which, if it hath, then Moses is content.

Now, this is the righteousness with which the Christian, as to justification, is made righteous; to wit, a righteousness that is neither essential to his Godhead, nor to his manhood; but such as standeth in that glorious person (who was such) his obedience to the law. Which righteousness himself had, with reference to himself, no need of at all, for his Godhead, yea, his manhood, was perfectly righteous without it. This righteousness therefore was there, and there only necessary, where Christ was considered as God's servant (and our surety) to bring to God Jacob again, and to restore the preserved of Israel. For though Christ was a Son, yet he became a servant to do, not for himself, for he had no need, but for us, the whole law, and so bring in everlasting righteousness for us.

And hence it is said, that Christ did what he did for us. He became the end of the law for righteousness for us; he suffered for us, he died for us, he laid down his life for us, and he gave himself for us. The righteousness then that Christ did fulfil, when he was in the world, was not for himself simply considered, nor for himself personally considered, for he had no need thereof; but it was for the elect, the members of his body.

Christ then did not fulfil the law for himself, for he had no need thereof. Christ again did fulfil the law for himself, for he had need of the righteousness thereof; he had need thereof for the covering of his body, and the several members thereof; for they, in a good sense, are himself, members of his body, of his flesh, and of his bones; and he owns them as parts of himself in many places of the holy scriptures; Eph. v. 30; Acts ix. 4, 5; Matt. xxv. 45; x. 40; Mark ix. 37; Luke x. 16; 1 Cor. xii. 12, 27. This righteousness then, even the whole of what Christ did in answer to the law, it was for us; and God hath put it upon them, and they were righteous in it, even righteous as he is righteous. And this they have before they do acts of righteousness.

Secondly, There is righteousness put into them, before they act righteous things. A righteousness, I say, put into them; or I had rather that you should call it a principle of righteousness; for it is a principle of life to righteousness. Before man's conversion, there is in him a principle of death to sin; but when he is converted to Christ, there is put in him a principle of righteousness, that he may bring forth fruit unto God; Rom. vii. 4-6.

Hence they are said to be quickened, to be made alive, to be risen from death to life, to have the Spirit of God dwelling in them; not only to make their souls alive, but to quicken their mortal bodies to that which is good; Rom. viii. 11.

Here, as I hinted before, they that do righteousness are said to be born of him, that is, antecedent to their doing of righteousness, 1 John ii. 29; "born of him," that is, made alive with new, spiritual, and heavenly life. Wherefore the exhortation to them is, "Neither yield ye your members as instruments of unrighteousness unto sin; but yield yourselves unto God, as those that are alive from the dead, and your members as instruments of righteousness unto God;" Rom. vi. 13.

Now this principle must also be in men, before they can do that which is spiritual: for whatever seeming good thing any man doth, before he has bestowed upon him this heavenly principle from God, it is accounted nothing, it is accounted sin and abomination in the sight of God; for an evil tree cannot bring forth good fruit: "Men do not gather grapes of thorns; neither of a bramble gather figs." It is not the fruit that makes the tree, but the tree that makes the fruit. A man must be good, before he can do good; and evil before he can do evil.

This is that which is asserted by the Son of God himself; and it lieth so level with reason and the nature of things, that it cannot be contradicted: Matth. vii. 16-18; Luke vi. 43-45. "A good man, out of the good treasure of his heart, bringeth forth that which is good: and an evil man, out of the evil treasure of his heart, bringeth forth that which is evil." But notwithstanding all that can be said, it seemeth very strange to the carnal world; for they will not be otherwise persuaded, but that they be good deeds that make good men, and evil ones that make evil men. And so, by such dotish apprehensions, do what in them lieth to fortify their hearts with the mists of darkness against the clear shining of the word, and conviction of the truth.

And thus it was from the beginning. Abel's first services to God were from this principle of righteousness; but Cain would have been made righteous by his deeds; but his deeds not flowing from the same root of goodness, as did Abel's, notwithstanding he did it with the very best he had, is yet called evil: for he wanted, I say, the principles, to wit, of grace and faith, without which no action can be counted good in a gospel-sense.

These two things, then, that man must have that will do righteousness. He must have put upon him the perfect righteousness of Christ: and he must have that dwelling in him, as a fruit of the new birth, a principle of righteousness. Then indeed he is a tree of righteousness, and God is like to be glorified in and by him; but this the Pharisee was utterly ignorant of, and at the remotest distance from.

You may ask me next, But which of these are first bestowed upon the Christian--the perfect righteousness of Christ unto justification, or this gospel-principle of righteousness unto sanctification?

Answ. The perfect righteousness of Christ unto justification must first be made over to him by an act of grace. This is evident,

1. Because he is justified as ungodly; that is, whilst he is ungodly: but it must not be said of them that have this principle of grace in them, that they are ungodly; for they are saints and holy. But this righteousness, by it God justifieth the ungodly, by imputing it to them, when and while they, as to a principle of grace, are grace-less.

This is further manifested thus: The person must be accepted before his performance can; "And the Lord had respect unto Abel, and to his offering;" Gen. iv. If he had respect to Abel's person first, yet he must have respect unto it for the sake of some righteousness; but Abel as yet had no righteousness; for that he acted, after God had a respect unto his person. "And the Lord had respect unto Abel, and to his offering: but unto Cain, and to his offering, he had no respect."

The prophet Ezekiel also shews us this, where, by the similitude of the wretched infant, and of the manner of God's receiving it to mercy, he shews how he received the Jews to favour. First, saith he, "I spread my skirt over thee, and covered thy nakedness." There is justification; "I covered thy nakedness." But what manner of nakedness was it? Yes, it was then as naked as naked could be, even as naked as in the day that it was born; Ezek. xvi. 4-9. And as thus naked, it was covered, not with any thing but with the skirt of Christ; that is, with his robe of righteousness, with his obedience, that he performed of himself for that very purpose; for by the obedience of one, many are made righteous.

2. Righteousness unto justification must be first; because the first duty that a Christian performeth to God, must be accepted, not for the sake of the principle from which in the heart it flows, nor yet for the sake of the person that acts it, but for the sake of Christ, whose righteousness it is by which the sinner stands just before God. And hence it is said, "By faith Abel offered unto God a more excellent sacrifice than Cain," Heb. xi. By faith he did it; but faith in respect to the righteousness that justifies; for we are justified by faith; not by faith as it is an acting grace, but the righteousness of faith, that is, by that righteousness that faith embraceth, layeth hold of, and helpeth the soul to rest and trust to, for justification of life, which is the

obedience of Christ. Besides, it is said, by faith he offered; faith then in Christ was precedent to his offering.

Now, since faith was in act before his offer, and since before his offer he had no personal goodness of his own, faith must look out from home; I say to another for righteousness; and finding the righteousness of Christ to be the righteousness which by God was designed to be performed for the justification of a sinner, it embraces it, and through it offereth to God a more excellent sacrifice than Cain.

Hence it follows, "By which he obtained witness that he was righteous;" by which, not by his offering, but by his faith; for his offering, simply as an offering, could not have made him righteous if he had not been righteous before; for "an evil tree cannot bring forth good fruit." Besides, if this be granted, why had not God respect to Cain's offering as well as to Abel's? For did Abel offer? So did Cain. Did Abel offer his best? So did Cain his. And if with this we shall take notice of the order of their offspring, Cain seemed to offer first, and so with the frankest will and forwardest mind; but yet, saith the text, "The Lord had respect to Abel and to his offering." But why to Abel? Why, because his, person was made righteous before he offered his gift: "By which he obtained witness that he was righteous;" God testifying of his gifts, that they were good and acceptable because they declared Abel's acceptation of the righteousness of Christ, through the riches of the grace of God.

By faith, then, Abel offered to God a more excellent sacrifice than Cain. He shrouded himself under the righteousness of Christ, and so, of that righteousness, he offered to God. God also looking and finding him there (where he could not have been, as to his own apprehension, no otherwise than by faith), accepted of his gift; by which acceptation (for so you may understand it also) God testifieth that he was righteous, for God receiveth not the gifts and offerings of those that are not righteous, for their sacrifices are an abomination unto him, Prov. xxi. 27.

Abel then was, I say, made righteous, first, as he stood ungodly in himself; God justifieth the ungodly, Rom. iv. Now, being justified, he was righteous; and being righteous, he offered his sacrifice of praise to God, or other offerings which God accepted, because he believed in his Son. But this our Pharisee understandeth not.

3. Righteousness by imputation must be first, because we are made so, to wit, by another--"By the obedience of one shall many be made righteous." Now to be made righteous, implies a passiveness in him that is so made, and the activity of

the work to lie in some body else; except he had said, they had made themselves righteous; but that it doth not, nor doth the text leave to any the least countenance so to insinuate; nay, it plainly affirms the contrary, for it saith, by the obedience of one, of one man, Jesus Christ, many are made righteous; by the righteousness of one, Rom. v. So then, if they be made righteous by the righteousness of one; I say if many be made righteous by the righteousness of one, then are they that are so, as to themselves, passive and not active, with reference to the working out of this righteousness. They have no hand in that; for that is the act of one, the righteousness of one, the obedience of one, the workmanship of one, even of Christ Jesus.

Again, If they are made righteous by this righteousness, then also they are passive as to their first privilege by it; for they are made righteous by it; they do not make themselves righteous by it.

Imputation is also the act of God. "Even as David also describeth the blessedness of the man, unto whom God imputeth righteousness." The righteousness then is a work of Christ, his own obedience to his Father's law; the making of it ours is the act of the Father, and of his infinite grace: "For of him are ye in Christ Jesus, who of God is made unto us wisdom and righteousness." "For God hath made Jim to be sin for us, who knew no sin, that we might be made the righteousness of God in him." And both these things God shewed to our first parents, when he acted in grace towards them after the fall.

There it is said, the Lord God made unto Adam, and unto his wife, coats of skins, and clothed them; Gen. iii. 21.

Whence note,

(1.) That Adam and his wife were naked, both in God's eye and in their own, verses 10, 11.

(2.) That the Lord God made coats of skins.

(3.) That in his making of them, he had respect to Adam and to his wife, that is, he made them.

(4.) That when he had made them, he also clothed them therewith.

They made not the coats, nor did God bid them make them; but God did make them himself to cover their nakedness with. Yea, when he had made them, he did not bid them put them on, but he himself did clothe them with them: for thus runs the text; "Unto Adam also, and to his wife, did the Lord God make coats of skins, and clothed them." O it was the Lord God that made this coat with which a poor sinner is made righteous! And it is also the Lord God that putteth it upon us. But this our Pharisee understandeth not.

But now, if a man is not righteous before he is made so, before the Lord God has by the righteousness of another made him so; then whether this righteousness comes first or last, the man is not righteous until it cometh; and if he be not righteous until it cometh, then what works soever are done before it comes, they are not the works of a righteous man, nor the fruits of a good tree, but of a bad. And so again, this righteousness must first come before a man be righteous, and before a man does righteousness. Make the tree good, and its fruit will be good.

Now, since a man must be made righteous before he can do righteousness, it is manifest his works of righteousness do not make him righteous, no more than the fig makes its own tree a fig-tree, or than the grape doth make its own vine a vine. Hence those acts of righteousness that Christian men do perform, are called the fruits of righteousness, which are by Jesus Christ to the glory and praise of God; Phil. i. 11.

The fruits of righteousness they are by Jesus Christ, as the fruits of the tree are by the tree itself; for the truth is, that principle of righteousness, of which mention has been made before, and concerning which I have said it comes in in the second place; it is also originally to be found for us nowhere but in Christ.

Hence it is said to be by Jesus Christ; and again, "Of his fulness have we all received, and grace for grace;" John i. 16. A man must then be united to Christ first, and so being united, he partaketh of this benefit, to wit, a principle that is supernatural, spiritual, and heavenly. Now, his being united to Christ, is not of or from himself, but of and from the Father, who, as to this work, is the husbandman; even as the twig that is grafted into the tree officiateth not, that is, grafteth not itself thereunto, but is grafted in by some other, itself being utterly passive as to that. Now, being united unto Christ, the soul is first made partaker of justification, or of justifying righteousness, and now no longer beareth the name of an ungodly man; for he is made righteous by the obedience of Christ; he being also united to Christ, partaketh of the root and fatness of Christ; the root, that is, his divine nature; the fatness, that is, the fulness of grace that is laid up in him to be communicated unto us, even as the branch that is grafted into the olive-tree partaketh of the root and fatness of the olive-tree. Now partaking thereof, it quickeneth, it groweth, it bud-deth, and yieldeth fruit to the praise and glory of God; Rom. xi. 17.

But these things, as I have often said, the poor Pharisee was ignorant of, when so swaggeringly he, with his "God, I thank thee," came into the temple to pray. And, indeed, in that which hath been said is something of the mystery of God's will in his way with his elect; and such a mystery it is, that it lieth hid for ever to nature and natural men; for they think of nothing less than of this, nor of nothing more, when they think of their souls and of salvation, than that something must be done by themselves to reconcile them to God. Yea, if through some common convictions their understandings should be swayed to a consenting to that, that justification is of grace by Christ, and not of works by men; yet conscience, reason, and the law of nature, not being as yet subdued by the power and glory of grace unto the obedi-ence of Christ, will rise up in rebellion against this doctrine, and will over-rule and bow down the soul again to the law and works thereof for life.

4. Righteousness by imputation must be first, because, else faith, which is a part, yea, a greater part of that which is called a principle of grace in the soul, will have nothing to fix itself upon, nor a motive to work by. Let this therefore be con-sidered by those that are on the contrary side.

1. Faith, so soon as it has a being in the soul, is like the child that has a being in the mother's lap; it must have something to feed upon; not something at a distance, afar off, to be purchased (I speak now as to justification from the curse), but some-thing by promise made over of grace to the soul; something to feed upon to support from the fears of perishing by the curse for sin. Nor can it rest content with all du-ties and performances that other graces shall put the soul upon; nor with any of its own works, until it reaches and takes hold of the righteousness of Christ. Faith is like the dove, which found no rest any where until it returned to Noah into the ark. But this our Pharisee understandeth not.

Perhaps some may object, that from this way of reasoning it is apparent, that sanctification is first; since the soul may have faith, and so a principle of grace in it, and yet, as yet it cannot find Christ to feed and refresh the soul withal.

Answ. From this way of reasoning it is not at all apparent that sanctification, or a principle of grace, is in the soul before righteousness is imputed and the soul made perfectly righteous thereby. And for the clearing up of this, let me propose a few things.

1. Justifying righteousness, to wit, the obedience of that one man, Christ, is imputed to the sinner, to justify him in God's sight; for his law calls for perfect righteousness, and before that be come to, and put upon the poor sinner, God cannot bestow other spiritual blessings upon him; because by the law he has pronounced him accursed; by the which curse he is also so holden, until a righteousness shall be found upon the sinner, that the law and divine justice can approve of, and be contented within. So then, as to the justification of the sinner, there must be a righteousness for God; I say, for the sinner, and for God: for the sinner to be clothed within, and for God to look upon, that he may, for the sake thereof in a way of justice, bless the sinner with forgiveness of sins: for forgiveness of sins is the next thing that followeth upon the appearance of the sinner before God in the righteousness of Christ; Rom. iv. 6, 7.

Now, upon this forgiveness follows the second blessing. Christ hath redeemed us from the curse of the law, being made a curse for us; and so, consequently, hath obtained for us the forgiveness of sins: for he that is delivered from the curse hath received forgiveness of sins, or rather is made partaker thereof. Now, being made a partaker thereof, the second blessing immediately follows, to wit, the blessing of Abraham, that is, the promise of the Spirit through faith; Gal. iii. 13. 14. But this our Pharisee understandeth not.

But now, although it be of absolute necessity that imputed righteousness be first, to the soul; that is, that perfect righteousness be found upon the sinner first by God, that he may bestow other blessings in a way of justice:

Let God then put the righteousness of his Son upon me; and by virtue of that, let the second blessing of God come into me; and by virtue of that, let me be made to see myself a sinner, and Christ's righteousness, and my need of it, in the doctrine of it, as it is revealed in the scriptures of truth. Let me then believe this doctrine to be true, and be brought by my belief to repentance for my sins, to hungering and thirsting vehemently after this righteousness: for this is the kingdom of God, and his righteousness. Yea, let me pray, and cry, and sigh, and groan, day and night, to the God of this righteousness, that he will of grace make me a partaker. And let me thus be prostrate before my God, all the time that in wisdom he shall think fit; and in his own time he shall shew me that I am a justified person, a pardoned person, a person in whom the Spirit of God hath dwelt for some time, though I knew it not.

So then, justification before God is one thing, and justification in mine own eyes is another; not that these are two justifications, but the same righteousness by which I stand justified before God, may be seen of God, when I am ignorant of it: yea, for the sake of it I may be received, pardoned, and accounted righteous of him, and yet I may not understand it. Yea, further, he may proceed in the way of blessing to bless me with additional blessings, and yet I be ignorant of it.

So that the question is not, Do I find that I am righteous? but, Am I so? Doth God find me so, when he seeth that the righteousness of his Son is upon me, being made over to me by an act of his grace? For I am justified freely by his grace, through the redemption which is in Jesus Christ, whom God hath set forth to be a propitiation through faith in his blood, to declare his righteousness for the remission of sins that are past, through the forbearance of God; Rom. iii. 24. But this our Pharisee understandeth not.

I am then made righteous first by the righteousness of another; and because I am thus righteous, God accepteth of my person as such, and bestoweth upon me his grace; the which, at first, for want of skill and experience in the word of righteousness, I make use of but poorly, and have need to be certified that I am made righteous, and that I have eternal life; not by faith first and immediately, but by the written word which is called "the word of faith;" which word declareth unto me (to whom grace, and so faith in the seed of it, is given), that I have eternal life, and that I should with boldness, in peace and joy, believe on the Son of God; Heb. v. 13; Rom. xv. 13; 1 John v. 13. But,

Again, I, in the first acts of my faith, when I come at Christ, do not accept of him, because I know I am righteous, either with imputed righteousness, or with that which is inherent. Both these, as to my present privilege in them, may be hidden from mine eyes, and I only put upon taking of encouragement to close with Christ for life and righteousness, as he is set forth to be a propitiation before mine eyes, in the word of the truth of the gospel; to which word I adhere as, or because I find, I want peace with God in my soul, and because I am convinced that the means of peace is not to be found any where but in Jesus Christ. Now, by my thus adhering to him, I find stay for my soul, and peace to my conscience, because the word doth ascertain to me, that he that believeth on him hath remission of sins, hath eternal life, and shall be saved from the wrath to come.

But, alas! who knows (the many straits, and as I may say, the stress of weather, I mean) the cold blasts of hell, with which the poor soul is assaulted, betwixt its receiving of grace, and its sensible closing with Jesus Christ? None, I dare say, but it and its fellows. "The heart knows its own bitterness; and a stranger intermeddleth not with his joy;" Prov. xiv. 10. No sooner doth Satan perceive what God is doing with the soul, in a way of grace and mercy, but he endeavoureth what he may to make the renewing thereof bitter and wearisome work to the sinner. O what mists, what mountains, what clouds, what darkness, what objections, what false apprehensions of God, of Christ, of grace, of the word, and of the soul's condition, doth he now lay before it, and haunt it with; whereby he dejecteth, casteth down, daunteth, distresseth, and almost driveth it quite into despair! Now, by the reason of these things, faith (and all the grace that is in the soul) is hard put to it to come at the promise, and by the promise of Christ; as it is said, when the tempest and great danger of shipwreck lay upon the vessel in which Paul was, they had "much work to come by the boat;" Acts xxvii. 16. For Satan's design is, if he cannot keep the soul from Christ, to make his coming to him, and closing with him, as hard, as difficult and troublesome, as he by his devices can. But faith, true justifying faith, is a grace, is not weary by all that Satan can do; but meditateth upon the word, and taketh stomach, and courage, fighteth and crieth, and by crying and fighting, by help from heaven, its way is made through all the oppositions that appear so mighty, and draweth up at last to Jesus Christ, into whose bosom it putteth the soul, where, for the time, it sweetly resteth, after its marvellous tossings to and fro.

And besides what hath been said, let me yet illustrate this truth unto you by this familiar similitude.

Suppose a man, a traitor, that by the law should die for his sin, is yet such an one that the king has exceeding kindness for; may not the king pardon this man of his clemency; yea, order that his pardon should be drawn up and sealed, and so in every sense be made sure; and yet, for the present, keep all this close enough from the ears or the knowledge of the person therein concerned? Yea, may not the king after all leave this person, with others under the same transgression, to sue for and obtain this pardon with great expense and difficulty, with many tears and heart-achings, with many fears and dubious cogitations?

Why, this is the case between God and the soul that he saveth; he saveth him, pardoneth him, and secureth him from the curse and death that is due unto sin, but yet doth not tell him so; but he ascends in his great suit unto God for it. Only this difference we must make between God and the potentates of this world; God cannot pardon before the sinner stands before him righteous by the righteousness of Christ; because he has in judgment, and justice, and righteousness, threatened and concluded, that he that wants righteousness shall die.

And I say again, because this righteousness is God's and at God's disposal only, it is God that must make a man righteous before he can forgive him his sins, or bestow upon him of his secondary blessings; to wit, his Spirit, and the graces thereof. And I say again, it must be this righteousness; for it can be no other that justifies a sinner from sin in the sight of God, and from the sentence of the law.

Secondly, This is, and must be the way of God with the sinner, that faith may not only have an object to work upon, but a motive to work by.

(1.) Here, as I said, faith hath an object to work upon, and that in the person of Christ, and that personal righteousness of his, which he in the days of his flesh did finish to justify sinners withal. This is, I say, the object of faith for justification, whereunto the soul by it doth continually resort. Hence David saith to Christ, "Be thou my strong habitation (or as you have it in the margin, Be thou to me a rock of habitation) whereunto I may continually resort;" Psalm lxxi. 3. And two things he infers by so saying.

The first is, That the Christian is a man under continual exercises, sometimes one way, and sometimes another; but all his exercises have a tendency in them more or less to spoil him; therefore he is rather for flying to Christ than for grappling with them in and by his own power.

The second is, that Christ is of God our shelter as to this very thing. Hence his name is said to be "a strong tower," and that the righteous run into it, and are safe, Prov. xviii. 10. That also of David in the fifty-sixth Psalm is very pregnant to this purpose; "Mine enemies," saith he, "would daily swallow me up; for they be many that fight against me, O thou Most High." And what then? Why, saith he, "I will trust in thee." Thus you see, faith hath an object to work upon to carry the soul unto, and to secure the soul in times of difficulty, and that object is Jesus Christ and his righteousness. But,

(2.) Again, as faith hath an object to work upon, so it hath a motive to work by; and that is the love of God in giving of Christ to the soul for righteousness. Nor is there any profession, religion, or duty and performance, that is at all regarded, where this faith, which by such means can work, is wanting. "For in Jesus Christ neither circumcision availeth any thing, nor uncircumcision, but faith which worketh by love" (so Gal. v. 6) acteth lovely; or, by faith whose fruit is love (though true faith hath love for its offspring) but faith which worketh by love, that is true, saving, justifying faith, as it beholdeth the righteousness of Christ as made over to the soul for justification; so it beholdeth love, love to be the cause of its so being made over.

It beholdeth love in the Father, in giving of his Son, and love in the Son, in giving of himself to be made soul-saving righteousness for me. And seeing it worketh by it, that is, it is stirred up to an holy boldness of venturing all eternal concerns upon Christ, and also to an holy, endeared, affecting love of him, for his sweet and blessed redeeming love. Hence the apostle saith, "The love of Christ constraineth us; because we thus judge, that if one died for all, then were all dead: and that he died for all, that they which live, should not henceforth live unto themselves, but unto him which died for them and rose again," 2 Cor. v. 14, 15.

Thus then is the heart united in affection and love to the Father and the Son, for the love that they have shewed to the poor sinner in their thus delivering him from the wrath to come. For by this love faith worketh, in sweet passions and pangs of love, to all that are thus reconciled, as this sinner seeth he is. The motive then, whereby faith worketh, both as to justification and sanctification, the great motive to them, I say, is love, the love of God, and the love of Christ: "We love him, because he first loved us." That is, when our faith hath told us so; for so are the words above, "We have known and believed the love that God hath to us." And then, "We love him, because he first loved us." And then, "This commandment have we from him, that he that loveth God, loveth his brother also," 1 John iv. 16-21. But this our poor Pharisee understandeth not. But,

5. Righteousness by imputation must be first, to cut off boasting from the heart, conceit, and lips of men. Wherefore he saith, as before, that we are justified freely by the grace of God, not through, or for the sake of an holy gospel-principle in us; but "through the redemption that is in Jesus Christ," &c. "Where is boasting

then? It is excluded. By what law? Of works? Nay, but by the law of faith." And this is the law of faith, by which we are justified as before; Rom. iii. 27, 28.

Nor can any man propound such an essential way to cut off boasting as this, which is of God's providing: For what is man here to boast of? No righteousness, nor yet of the application of it to his soul. The righteousness is Christ's, not the sinner's. The imputation is God's, not the sinner's. The cause of imputation is God's grace and love, not the sinner's works of righteousness. The time of God's imputing righteousness is when the sinner was a sinner, wrapped up in ignorance, and wallowing in his vanity; not when he was good, or when he was seeking of it; for his inward gospel-goodness is a fruit of the imputation of justifying righteousness. Where is boasting then? Where is our Pharisee then, with his brags of not being as other men are? It is excluded, and he with it, and the poor Publican taken into favour, that boasting might be cut off. "Not of works, lest any man should boast." There is no trust to be put in men; those that seem most humble, and that to appearance, and farthest off from pride, it is natural to them to boast; yea, now they have no cause to boast; for by grace are we saved through faith, and that not of ourselves, it is the gift of God. "Not of works, lest any man should boast."

But if man is so prone to boast, when yet there is no pound of boasting in him, nor yet in what he doth; how would he have boasted had he been permitted by the God of heaven to have done something, though that something had been but a very little something, towards his justification? But God has prevented boasting by doing as he has done; Eph. ii. 8, 9. Nay, the apostle addeth further (lest any man should boast), that as to good works, "We are God's workmanship, created in Christ Jesus unto good works, which God hath before ordained that we should walk in them; ver. 10. Can the tree boast, since it was God that made it such? Where is boasting then? "But of him are ye in Christ Jesus, who of God is made unto us wisdom, and righteousness, and sanctification, and redemption: that, according as it is written, he that glorieth, let him glory in the Lord;" 1 Cor. i. 30, 31. Where is boasting then? Where is our Pharisee then, with all his works of righteousness, and with his boasts of being better than his neighbours?

It may be said, If we should be justified for the sake of our inherent righteousness, since that righteousness is the gift of God, will it not follow that boasting is, in the occasion thereof, cut off?

Answ. No; for although the principle of inherent righteousness be the gift of God, yet it bringeth forth fruits by man, and through man; and so man having a hand therein, though he should have ever so little, he has an occasion offered him to boast. Yea, if a man should be justified before God by the grace, or the working of the grace of faith in him, he would have ground of occasion to boast; because faith, though it be the gift of God, yet as it acteth in man, takes man along with it in its so acting; yea, the acting of faith is as often attributed to the man by whom it is acted, and oftener, than to the grace itself. How then can it be, but that man must have a hand therein, and so a ground therein, or thereof to boast?

But now, since justification from the curse of the law before God lieth only and wholly in God's imputing of Christ's righteousness to a man, and that too, while the man to whom it is imputed is in himself wicked and ungodly, there is no room left for boasting before God, for that is the boasting intended; but rather an occasion given to shame and confusion of face, and to stop the mouth for ever, since justification comes in a way so far above him, so vastly without him, his skill, help, or what else soever; Ezek. xvi. 61-63.

6. Righteousness by imputation must be first, that justification may not be of debt, but of mercy and grace. This is evident from reason. It is meet that God should therefore justify us by a righteousness of his own, not of his own prescribing; for that he may do, and yet the righteousness be ours; but of his own providing, that the righteousness may be his. "Now to him that worketh is the reward not reckoned of grace, but of debt;" Rom. iv. 2-4. If I work for justifying righteousness, and that way get righteousness, my justification is not of grace, but of debt. God giveth it not unto me, but he oweth it unto me; so then it is no longer his, but mine: mine, not of grace, but of debt. And if so, then I thank him not for his remission of sins, nor for the kingdom of heaven, nor for eternal life; for if justifying righteousness is of debt, then when I have it, and what dependeth thereon, I have but mine own; that which God oweth to me.

Nor will it help at all to say, But I obtain it by God's grace in me; because that doth not cut off my works, nor prevent my having of a hand in my justifying righteousness.

Suppose I give a man materials, even all materials that are necessary to the completing of such or such a thing; yet if he worketh, though the materials be mine,

I am to him a debtor, and he deserveth a reward. Thou sayst, God has given thee his Spirit, his grace, and all other things that are necessary for the working up of a complete righteousness. Well, but is thy work required to the finishing of this righteousness? If so, this is not the righteousness that justifieth; because it is such as has thy hand, thy workmanship therein, and so obtains a reward. And observe it, righteousness, justifying righteousness, consisteth not in a principle of righteousness, but in works of righteousness; that is, in good duties, in obedience, in a walking in the law to the pleasing of the law, and the content of the justice of God.

I suppose again, that thou shalt conclude with me, that justifying righteousness, I mean that which justifies from the curse of the law, resideth only in the obedience of the Son of God; and that the principle of grace that is in thee is none of that righteousness, no, not then when thou hast to the utmost walked with God according to thy gift and grace; yet if thou concludest that this principle must be in thee, and these works done by thee, before this justifying righteousness is imputed to thee for justification, thou layest in a caveat against justification by grace; and also concludest, that though thou art not justified by thy righteousness, but by Christ, yet thou art justified by Christ's righteousness for the sake of thine own, and so makest justification to be still a debt. But here the scripture doth also cut thee off: "Not for thy righteousness, or for the uprightness of thine heart, dost thou go to possess the land" (which was but a type of heaven); and if our righteousness cannot give us, by its excellency, a share in the type, be sure that for it we shall never be sharers in the anti-type itself. "Understand, therefore, that the Lord thy God giveth thee not this good land to possess it for thy righteousness; for thou art a stiff-necked people;" Deut. ix. 5, 6.

Gospel-performances, therefore, are not first; that was first, for the sake of which God did receive these people into favour with himself, and that was a covenant-righteousness; and where could that covenant-righteousness be found, but in the Prince, Mediator, and High Priest of the covenant? For it was he, and he only, that was appointed of God, nor could any but himself bring in everlasting righteousness; Dan. ix. 24, 25. This is evident from these texts last mentioned; it was not for their righteousness that they possessed the land.

Again, As it was not for their righteousness that they were made possessors of the land, so it was not for the sake of their righteousness that they were made partakers of such a righteousness that did make them possess the land. This is plain to reason; for personal righteousness, when by us performed, is of no worth to obtain of God a justifying righteousness. But if it be of no worth to obtain a justifying righteousness, then, it seems, it is more commodious to both parties than justifying righteousness. First, it is more commodious to him that worketh it; and, secondly, it is more commodious unto him that receiveth it, else why doth he for it give us a due debt, and so put upon us the everlasting justifying righteousness?

Perhaps it will be objected, That God doth all this of grace; but I answer, That these are but fallacious words, spoken by the tongue of the crafty. For we are not now discoursing of what rewards God can give to the operations of his own grace in us, but whether he can in a way of justice (or how he will) bestow any spiritual blessing upon sinful creatures, against whom, for sin, he has pronounced the curse of the law, before he hath found them in a righteousness, that is proved to be as good justice and righteousness, as is the justice and righteousness of the law, with which we have to do.

I assert he cannot, because he cannot lie, because he cannot deny himself: for if he should first threaten the transgression of the law with death, and yet afterwards receive the transgressor to grace, without a plenary satisfaction, what is this but to lie, and to diminish his truth, righteousness, and faithfulness; yea, and also to over-throw the sanction and perfect holiness of his law? His mercy, therefore, must act so towards the sinner that justice may be satisfied, and that can never be without a justifying righteousness.

Now what this justifying righteousness should be, and when imputed, that is the question. I say, it is the righteousness, or obedience of the Son of God in the flesh, which he assumed, and so his own, and the righteousness of no body else otherwise than by imputation.

I say again, that this righteousness must be imputed first, that the sinner may stand just in God's sight from the curse, that God might deal with him both in a way of justice as well as mercy, and yet do the sinner no harm.

But you may ask, how did God deal with sinners before his righteousness was actually in being?

I answer, He did then deal with sinners even as he dealeth with them now; he justified them by it, by virtue of the suretyship of him that was to bring it in.

Christ became surety for us, and by his suretyship laid himself under an obligation for those for whom he became a surety to bring in this everlasting and justifying righteousness, and by virtue of this, those of his elect that came into and went out of the world before he came to perform his work were saved though the forbearance of God. Wherefore, before the Lord came, they were saved for the Lord's sake, and for the sake of his name. And they that were spiritually wise understood it, and pleaded it as their necessities required, and the Lord accepted them; Heb. vii. 22; Rom. iv. 24; Dan. ix. 17; Psalm xxv. 11.

7. Righteousness by imputation must be first, that justification may be certain; "Therefore it is of faith (of the righteousness that faith layeth hold on), that it might be by grace; to the end the promise might be sure to all the seed;" Rom. iv. 16. "That the promise,"--What promise? The promise of remission of sins, &c., might be sure.

Now a promise of remission of sins supposeth a righteousness going before; for there is no forgiveness of sins, nor promise of forgiveness, for the sake of righteousness that shall be by us, but that already found in Christ as head, and so imputed to the elect for their remission. "God for Christ's sake hath forgiven you," Eph. iv. 32; For Christ's sake; that this, for the sake of the righteousness of Christ. Imputed righteousness must be first; yea, it must be before forgiveness, and forgiveness is extended by God then when we lie in our blood, though to us it is manifested afterwards. Therefore it is OF faith; he saith not BY it, respecting the act of faith, but of, respecting the doctrine or word which presenteth me with this blessed imputed righteousness: they that are of faith are the children of faithful Abraham. They that are of the doctrine of faith, for all the elect are the sons of that doctrine in which is this righteousness of Christ contained; yea, they are begotten by it of God to this inheritance, to their comfortable enjoyment of the comfort of it by faith.

That the promise might be sure to all the seed, to all them wrapped up in the promise, and so begotten and born. That it might be sure, implying that there is no certain way of salvation for the elect but this; because God can never by other means reconcile us to himself, for his heavenly eyes perceive, yea, they spy faults in the best of our gospel performances; yea, our faith is faulty, and also imperfect: how then should remission be extended to us for the sake of that? But now the righteousness of Christ is perfect, perpetual and stable as the great mountains; wherefore he is called the rock of our salvation, because a man may as soon tumble the mountains before him, as sin can make invalid the righteousness of Christ, when, and unto whom, God shall impute it for justice; Psalm xxxvi. In the margin it is said to be like the mountain of God; to wit, called Mount Zion, or that Moriah on which the temple was built, and upon which it stood; all other bottoms are fickle, all other righteousnesses are so feeble, short, narrow, yea, so full of imperfections; for what the law could not do in that it was weak through the flesh, Christ did for us in the similitude of sinful- flesh. But what could not the law do? Why, it could not give us righteousness, nor strengthen us to perform it. It could not give us any certain, solid, well-grounded hope of remission of sin and salvation.

Wherefore this righteousness being imputed, justice findeth no fault therewith, but consenteth to the extending to the sinner those blessings that tend to perfect his happiness in the heavens.

8. Righteousness by imputation must be first, that in all things Christ may have the pre-eminence. Christ is head of the church, and therefore let him have the highest honour in the soul; but how can he have that, if any precede as to justification before his perfect righteousness be imputed? If it be said, grace may be in the soul, though the soul doth not act it until the moment that justifying righteousness shall be imputed:

I ask, What should it do there before, or to what purpose is it there, if it be not acted? And again, how came it thither, how got the soul possession of it while it was unjustified? or, How could God in justice give it to a person, that by the law stood condemned, before they were acquitted from that condemnation? And I say, nothing can set the soul free from that curse but the perfect obedience of Christ; nor that either, if it be not imputed for that end to the sinner by the grace of God.

Imputed, that is, reckoned or accounted to him. And why should it not be accounted to him for righteousness? What did Christ bring it into the world for? for the righteous or for sinners? No doubt for sinners. And how must it be reckoned to them? Not in circumcision, but in uncircumcision; not as righteous, but as sinners. And how are they to consider of themselves, even then when they first are apprehensive of their need of this righteousness? Are they to think that they are righteous, or sinners?

And again, How are they to believe concerning themselves, then when they put forth the first act of faith towards this righteousness for justification? Are they to think that they are righteous, or sinners? Sinners, doubtless, they are to reckon themselves, and as such to reckon themselves justified by this righteousness. And this is according to the sentence of God, as appeareth by such sayings.

"For when we were yet without strength, in due time Christ died for the ungodly."

"But God commendeth his love toward us, in that, while we were yet sinners, Christ died for us."

"For if, while we were enemies, we were reconciled to God by the death of his Son," &c., Rom. v.

Out of these words I gather these three things.

1. That Christ by God's appointment died for us.

2. That by his death he reconciled us to God.

3. That even then, when the very act of reconciliation was in performing, and also when performed, we were ungodly, sinners, enemies.

Now, the act by which we are said to be reconciled to God, while ungodly, while sinners, and while enemies, was Christ's offering himself a sacrifice for us, which is, in the words above mentioned, called his death. Christ died for the ungodly; Christ died for us while sinners; Christ reconciled us to God by his death. And as Christ is said to die for us, so the Father is said to impute righteousness to us; to wit, as we are without works, as we are ungodly. "Now to him that worketh not, but believeth on him that justifieth the ungodly, his faith is counted for righteousness." He worketh not, but is ungodly, when this gracious act of God, in imputing the righteousness of Christ to him, is extended; when he shall believe, his faith is counted to him for righteousness. And why should we not have the benefit of the righteousness, since it was completed for us while we were yet ungodly? Yea, we have the benefit of it: "For when we were enemies, we were reconciled to God by the death of his Son."

When I say the benefit, I mean that benefit that we are capable of, and that is justification before God; for that a man may be capable of while he is in himself ungodly, because this comes to him by the righteousness of another. True, were it to be his own righteousness by which he was to be justified, he could not: but the righteousness is Christ's, and that imputed by God, not as a reward for work, or of debt, but freely by his grace; and therefore may be, and is so, while the person concerned is without works, ungodly, and a sinner.

And he that denieth that we are capable of this benefit while we are sinners and ungodly, may with the like reason deny that we are created beings: for that which is done for a man without him, may be done for him at any time which they that do it shall appoint. While a man is a beggar, may not I make him worth ten thousand a-year, if I can and will: and yet he may not know thereof in that moment that I make him so? yet the revenue of that estate shall really be his from the moment that I make him so, and he shall know it too at the rent-day.

This is the case: we are sinners and ungodly; there is a righteousness wrought out by Jesus Christ which God hath designed we shall be made righteous by: and by it, if he will impute it to us, we shall be righteous in his sight; even then when we are yet ungodly in ourselves: for he justifies the ungodly.

Now, though it is irregular and blameworthy in man to justify the wicked, because he cannot provide and clothe him with a justifying righteousness, yet it is glorious, and for ever worthy of praise, for God to do it: because it is in his power, not only to forgive, but to make a man righteous, even then when he is a sinner, and to justify him while he is ungodly.

But it may be yet objected, that though God has received satisfaction for sin, and so sufficient terms of reconciliation by the obedience and death of his Son, yet he imputeth it not unto us, but upon condition of our becoming good.

Ans. This must not be admitted: For,

1. The scripture saith not so; but that we are reconciled to God by the death of his Son, and justified too, and that while or when we are sinners and ungodly.

2. If this objection carrieth truth in it, then it follows that the Holy Ghost, faith, and so all grace, may be given to us, and we may have it dwelling in us, yea, acting in us, before we stand righteous in the judgment of the law before God (for nothing can make us stand just before God in the judgment of the law, but the obedience of the Son of God without us.) And if the Holy Ghost, faith, and so, consequently, the habit of every grace, may be in us, acting in us, before Christ's righteousness be by God imputed to us, then we are not justified as sinners and ungodly, but as persons inherently holy and righteous before.

But I have shewed you that this cannot be, therefore righteousness for justification must be imputed first. And here let me present the reader with two or three things.

1. That justification before God is one thing, and justification to the understanding and conscience is another. Now, I am treating of justification before God, not of it as to man's understanding and conscience: and I say, a man may be justified before God, even then when himself knoweth nothing thereof; Isa. xl. 2; Mark ii. 5; and while he hath not faith about it, but is ungodly.

2. There is justification by faith, by faith's applying of that righteousness to the understanding and conscience, which God hath of his grace imputed for righteousness to the soul for justification in his sight. And this is that by which we, as to sense and feeling, have peace with God "Being justified by faith, we have peace with God, through our Lord Jesus Christ;" Rom. v. 1. And these two the apostle keepeth distinct in the 10th verse: that "while we were enemies we were reconciled to God by the death of his Son." He addeth, "And not only so, but we joy in God through our Lord Jesus Christ, by whom we have now received the atonement," verse 11. Here you see, that to be reconciled to God by the death of his Son is one thing, and for us actually to receive by faith this reconciliation is another: and not only so, but we have "received the atonement."

3. Men do not gather their justification from God's single act of imputing of righteousness, that we might stand clear in his sight from the curse and judgment of the law; but from the word of God, which they understand not till it is brought to their understanding by the light and glory of the Holy Ghost.

We are not, therefore, in the ministry of the word to pronounce any man justified, from a supposition that God has imputed righteousness to him (since that act is not known to us), until the fruits that follow thereupon do break out before our eyes; to wit, the signs and effects of the Holy Ghost indwelling in our souls. And then we may conclude it, that is, that such a one stands justified before God, yet not for the sake of his inherent righteousness, nor yet for the fruits thereof, and so not for the sake of the act of faith, but for the sake of Jesus Christ his doing and suffering for us.

Nor will it avail to object, that if at first we stand justified before God by his imputing of Christ's righteousness unto us, though faith be not in us to act, we may always stand justified so; and so what need of faith? for therefore are we justified, first, by the imputation of God, as we are ungodly, that thereby we may be made capable of receiving the Holy Ghost and his graces in a way of righteousness and justice. Besides, God will have those that he shall justify by his grace through the redemption that is in Jesus Christ to have the Holy Ghost, and so faith, that they may know and believe the things not only that shall be, but that already are freely given to us of God. "Now," says Paul, "we have received, not the spirit of the world but the Spirit which is of God, that we might know the things that are freely given to us of God;" 1 Cor. ii. 12. To know, that is, to believe: it is given to you to believe, who believe according to the working of his mighty power; "And we have known and believed the love that God hath to us," preceding to our believing; John iv. 16. He then that is justified by God's imputation, shall believe by the power of the Holy Ghost; for that must come, and work faith, and strengthen the soul to act it, because imputed righteousness has gone before. He then that believeth shall be saved; for his believing is a sign, not a cause, of his being made righteous before God by impu-tation; and he that believeth not shall be damned.

AND THUS MUCH FOR THE PHARISEE, AND FOR HIS INFORMATION. AND NOW I COME TO THAT PART OF THE TEXT WHICH REMAINS, AND WHICH RESPECTETH THE PUBLICAN.

"And the Publican, standing afar off, would not lift up so much as his eyes unto heaven, but smote upon his breast, saying, God be merciful to me a sinner."

What this Publican was, I have shewed you, both with respect to nation, office, and disposition. Wherefore I shall not here trouble the reader as to that. We now, therefore, come to his repentance in the whole and in the parts of it; concerning which I shall take notice of several things, some more remote, and some more near to the matter and life of it.

But, first, let us see how cross the Pharisee and the Publican did lie in the temple one to another, while they both were presenting of their prayers to God.

1. The Pharisee he goes in boldly, fears nothing, but trusteth in himself that his state is good, that God loves him, and that there was no doubt to be made but of his good speed in this his religious enterprise. But, alas! poor Publican, he sneaks, crawls into the temple, and when he comes there, stands behind, aloof, off; as one not worthy to approach the divine presence.

2. The Pharisee at his approach hath his mouth full of many fine things, where-

by he strokes himself over the head, and in effect calls himself one of God's dear sons, that always kept close to his will, abode with him, or, as the prodigal's brother said, "Lo, these many years do I serve thee; neither transgressed I at any time thy commandment;" Luke xv. 29. But alas! poor Publican, thy guilt, as to these pleas, stops thy mouth; thou hast not one good thing to say of thyself, not one rag of righteousness; thy conscience tells thee so; yea, and if thou shouldst now attempt to set a good face on it, and for thy credit say something after the Pharisee in way of thine own commendations, yet here is God on the one side, the Pharisee on the other, together with thine own heart, to give thee a check, to rebuke thee, to condemn thee, and to lay thee even to the ground for thy insolence.

3. The Pharisee in his approach to God, wipes his fingers of the Publican's enormities, will not come nigh him, lest he should defile himself with his beastly rags: "I am not as other men are, nor yet as this Publican." But the poor Publican, alas for him! his fingers are not clean, nor can he tell how to make them so; besides, he meekly and quietly puts up with this reflection of the Pharisee upon him, and by silent behaviour justifies the severe sentence of that self-righteous man, concluding with him, that for his part he is wretched, and miserable, and poor, and blind, and naked, and not worthy to come nigh, or to stand by, so good, so virtuous, so holy, and so deserving a man as our sparkling Pharisee is.

4. The Pharisee, as at feasts and synagogues, chose the chief and first place for his person, and for his prayer, counting that the Publican was not meet, ought not to presume to let his foul breath once come out of his polluted lips in the temple, till HE had made his holy prayer. And, poor Publican, how dost thou hear and put up this with all other affronts, counting even as the Pharisee counted of thee, that thou wast but a dog in comparison of him, and therefore not fit to go before, but to come as in chains, behind, and forbear to present thy mournful supplication to the holy God, till he had presented his, in his own conceit, brave, gay, and fine oration?

5. The Pharisee, as he is numerous in his repeating his good deeds, so is he stiff in standing to them, bearing up himself, that he hath now sufficient foundation on which to bear up his soul against all the attempts of the law, the devil, sin, and hell. But, alas, poor Publican! thou standest naked, nay, worse than naked; for thou art clothed with filthy garments, thy sins cover thy face with shame: nor hast thou in, or of thyself, any defence from, or shelter against, the attempts, assaults, and cen-

sures of thy spiritual enemies, but art now in thine own eyes (though in the temple) cast forth into thine open field stark-naked, to the loathing of thy person, as in the day that thou wast born, and there ready to be devoured and torn in pieces for thy transgressions against thy God.

What wilt thou do, Publican? What wilt thou do? Come, let us see; which way wilt thou begin to address thyself to God? Bethink thyself: hast thou any thing to say? speak out, man: the Pharisee by this time has done, and received his sentence: make an "O yes;" let all the world be silent; yea, let the angels of heaven draw near and listen; for the Publican is come to have to do with God! yea, is come from the receipt of custom into the temple to pray to him.

"And the Publican, standing afar off, would not lift up so much as his eyes unto heaven, but smote upon his breast, saying, God be merciful to me a sinner." And is this thy way, poor Publican! O cunning sinner! O crafty Publican! thy wisdom has outdone the Pharisee; for it is better to apply ourselves to God's mercy than to trust to ourselves that we are righteous. But that the Publican did hit the mark, yea, get nearer unto, and more in the heart of God and his Son than the Pharisee, the sequel will make manifest.

Take notice then of this profound speech of the Publican, "God be merciful to me a sinner." Yea, the Son of God was so delighted with this prayer, that for the sake of it, he even as a limner draweth out the Publican in his manner of standing, behaviour, gestures, &c., while he makes this prayer to God: wherefore we will take notice both of the one and of the other; for surely his gestures put lustre into his prayer and repentance.

1. His prayer you see is this, "God be merciful to me a sinner."

His gestures in his prayer were in general three.

1. He "stood afar off."

2. He "would not lift up so much as his eyes to heaven."

3. He "smote upon his breast," with his fist, saying, "God be merciful to me a sinner."

To begin first with his prayer. In this prayer we have two things to consider of.

1. His confession: I am a sinner.

2. His imploring of help against this malady: "God be merciful to me a sin-

ner."

In his confession divers things are to be taken notice of. As -

1. The fairness and simplicity of his confession; "A sinner:" I am a sinner; "God be merciful to me a sinner." This indeed he was, and this indeed he confesses; and this, I say, he doth of godly simplicity. For a man to confess himself a sinner, it is to speak all against himself that can be spoken. And man, as degenerate, is too much an hypocrite, and too much a self-flatterer, thus to confess against himself, unless made simple and honest through the power of conviction upon his heart. And it is worth your noting, that he doth not say he was, or had been, but that at that time his state was such, to wit, a sinner. "God be merciful to me a sinner," or who am, and now stand before thee a sinner, in my sins.

Now, a little to shew you what it is to be a sinner; for every one that sinneth may not in a proper sense be called a sinner. Saints, the sanctified in Christ Jesus, do often sin, but it is not proper to call them sinners: but here the Publican calls himself a sinner; and therefore in effect calls himself an evil tree, one that beareth no good fruit; one whose body and soul is polluted, whose mind and conscience is defiled; one who hath walked according to the course of this world, and after the spirit that now worketh in the children of disobedience: they having their minds at enmity against God, and are taken captive by the devil at his will; a sinner, one whose trade hath been in sin, and the works of Satan all his days.

Thus he waives all pleas, and stoops his neck immediately to the block. Though he was a base man, yet he might have had pleas; pleas, I say, as well as the Pharisee, though not so many, yet as good. He was of the stock of Abraham, a Jew, an Israelite of the Israelites, and so a privileged man in the religion of the Jews, else what doth he do in the temple? Yea, why did not the Pharisee, if he was a heathen, lay that to his charge while he stood before God? But the truth is, he could not; for the Publican was a Jew as well as the Pharisee, and consequently might, had he been so disposed, have pleaded that before God. But he would not, he could not, for his conscience was under convictions, the awakenings of God were upon him; wherefore his privileges melt away like grease, and fly from him like the chaff of the summer threshing-floor, which the wind taketh up and scattereth as the dust; he therefore lets all privileges fall, and pleads only that he us a sinner.

2. In this confession he judges and condemns himself: For a man to say, I am

a sinner, is as much as to say, I am contrary to the holiness of God, a transgressor of the law, and consequently an object of the curse, and an heir of hell. The Publican, therefore, goeth very far in this his confession; For,

3. In the third place, To confess that there is nothing in him, done or can be done by him, that should allure, or prevail with God to do any thing for him: for a sinner cannot do good; no, not work up his heart unto one good thought: no, though he should have heaven itself if he could, or was sure to burn in hell-fire for ever and ever if he could not. For sin, where it is in possession, and bears rule, as it doth in every one that we may properly call a sinner, there it hath the mastery of the man, hath bound up his senses in cords and chains, and made nothing so odious to the soul as the things that are of the Spirit of God. Wherefore it is said of such, that they are "Enemies in their minds;" that "The carnal mind is enmity against God," and that "Wickedness proceedeth of the wicked;" and that the Ethiopian may as well change his skin, or the leopard his spots, as they that are accustomed to do evil may learn to do well; Col. i.; Rom. viii.; 1 Sam. xxiv. 13; Jer. xiii. 23.

4. In this confession he implicitly acknowledgeth that sin is the worst of things, forasmuch as it layeth the soul out of the reach of all remedy that can be found under heaven. Nothing below or short of the mercy of God can deliver a poor soul from this fearful malady. This the Pharisee did not see. Doubtless he did conclude, that at some time or other he had sinned; but he never in all his life did arrive to a sight of what sin was: his knowledge of it was but false and counterfeit, as is manifest by his cure; to wit, his own righteousness. For take this for a truth undeniable, that he that thinks himself better before God, because of his reformations, never yet had the true knowledge of his sin: But the poor Publican he had it, he had it in truth, as is manifest, because it drives him to the only sovereign remedy. For indeed, the right knowledge of sin, in the filth, and guilt, and damning power thereof, makes a man to understand, that not any thing but grace and mercy by Christ can secure him from the hellish ruins thereof.

Suppose a man sick of an apoplexy unto death, and should for his remedy make use only of those things that are good against the second ague, would not this demonstrate that this man was not sensible of the nature and danger of this disease? The same may be said of every sinner that shall make use only of those means to justify him before God, that can hardly make him go for a good Christian before judicious men. But the poor Publican, he knew the nature and the danger of his disease; and knew also, that nothing but mercy, infinite mercy, could cure him thereof.

5. This confession of the Publican declareth, that he himself was borne up now by an almighty though invisible hand. For sin, when seen in its colours, and when appearing in its monstrous shape, frighteth all away from God. This is manifest by Cain, Judas, Saul, and others, who could not stand up before God under the sense and appearance of their sin, but fled before him, one to one fruit of despair, and one to another. But now this Publican, though he apprehends his sin, that himself was one that was a sinner, yet he beareth up, cometh into the temple, approaches the presence of an holy and sin-revenging God, stands before him, and confesses that he is that man that sin had defiled, and that had brought him into the danger of damnation thereby.

This therefore was a mighty act of the Publican. He went against the voice of conscience, against sense and feeling, against the curse and condemning verdict of the law: he went, as I may say, upon hot burning coals to one that to sin and sinners is a consuming fire.

Now then, did the Publican this of his own head, or from his own mind? No, verily; there was some super-natural power within that did secretly prompt him on, and strengthen him to this more noble venture. True, there is nothing more common among wicked men, than to trick and toy, and play with this saying of the Publican, "God be merciful to me a sinner:" not at all being sensible either what sin is, or of their need of mercy. And such sinners shall find their speed in the Publican's prayer far otherwise than the Publican sped himself; it will happen unto them much as it happened unto the vagabond Jews, exorcists, who took upon them to call over them that had evil spirits, the name of the Lord Jesus; that were beaten by that spirit, and made fly out of that house naked and wounded, Acts xix. 13. Poor sinner, thou wilt say the Publican's prayer, and make the Publican's confession, and say, "God be merciful to me a sinner." But hold; dost thou do it with the Publican's heart, sense, dread, and simplicity? If not, thou dost but abuse the Publican and his prayer, and thyself and his God; and shalt find God rejecting of thee and thy prayers, saying, The Publican I know; his prayers and godly tears I know; but who or what art thou? and will send thee away naked. They are the hungry that he filleth with good things, but the rich (and the senseless) he sendeth empty away.

For my part, I find it one of the hardest things that I can put my soul upon, even to come to God, when warmly sensible that I am a sinner, for a share in grace and mercy. Oh! methinks it seems to me as if the whole face of the heavens were set against me. Yea, the very thought of God strikes me through; I cannot bear up, I cannot stand before him; I cannot but with a thousand tears say, "God be merciful to me a sinner;" Ezra ix. 15.

At another time, when my heart is more hard and stupid, and when his terror doth not make me afraid, then I can come before him, and ask mercy at his hand, and scarce be sensible of sin or grace, or that indeed I am before God. But above all, they are the rare times, when I can go to God as the Publican, sensible of his glorious majesty, sensible of my misery, and bear up, and affectionately cry, "God me merciful to me a sinner."

But again, the Publican, by his confession, sheweth a piece of the highest wisdom that a mortal man can shew; because; by so doing, he engageth as well as imploreth the grace and mercy of God to save him. You see by the text he imploreth it; and now I will shew you that he engageth it, and makes himself a sharer in it.

"He that covereth his sins shall not prosper; but whoso confesseth and forsaketh them shall have mercy." And again, "If we confess our sins, he is faithful and just to forgive us our sins and to cleanse us from all unrighteousness;" Prov. xxviii. 13; 1 John. i. 9.

First, In the promise of pardon, "he shall have mercy;" he shall have his sins forgiven. As also Solomon prays, that God will forgive them that know their own sores; and they are indeed such as are sensible of the plague of their own heart, 2 Chron. vi. 29, 30; 1 Kings viii. 37, 38. And the reason is, because the sinner is now driven to the farthest point, for confession is the farthest point, and the utmost bound unto which God has appointed the Publican to go, with reference to his work; as it is said of Saul to David, when he was about to give him Michal his daughter to wife, "I desire not any dowry, but an hundred foreskins of the Philistines, to be avenged of the king's enemies."

So says God in this matter, I desire no sacrifices, nor legal righteousness to make thee acceptable to me: "Only acknowledge and confess thine iniquity, that thou hast transgressed against me," 1 Sam. xviii. 25; Jer. iii. 12, 13. And though this by some may be thought to be a very easy way to come at, and partake of the mercy of God; yet let the sensible sinner try it, and he shall find it one of the hardest things in the world. And there are two things to which man is prone, that makes confession hard:

First, There is a great proneness in us to be partial, and not thorough and plain in our confessions. We are apt to make half confessions; to confess some, and hide some; or else to make feigned confessions, flattering both ourselves, and also God, while we make confession unto him; or else to confess sin, as our own fancies apprehend, and not as the word descries them. These things we are very prone to do; men can confess little sins, while they hide great ones. Men can feign themselves sorry for sin when they are not, or else in their confessions forget to judge of sin by the word. Hence it is said, They turned to God, "not with their whole hearts, but as it were feignedly." "They spake not aright, saying, What have I done?" "They flatter him with their mouth, and lie unto him with their tongues," and do their wickedness in the dark, and sin against him with a high hand, and then come to him and "cover the altar with their tears." These things therefore demonstrate the difficulty of sincere confession of sin; and that to do it as it should, is no such easy thing.

To right confession of sin, several things must go: as,

1. There must be sound conviction for sin upon the spirit: for before a man shall be convinced of the nature, aggravation, and evil of sin, how shall he make godly confession of it? Now, to convince the soul of sin, the law must be set home upon the conscience by the Spirit of God: "For by the law is the knowledge of sin." And again, "I had not known lust, unless the law had said, Thou shalt not covet;" Rom. vii. 7. This law, now when it effectually ministereth conviction--of sin to the conscience, doth it by putting of life, and strength, and terror into sin. By its working on the conscience, it makes sin revive, "and the strength of sin is the law;" Rom. vii.; 1 Cor. xv. It also increaseth and multiplieth sin, both by the revelation of God's anger against the soul, and also by mustering up and calling to view sins committed and forgotten time out of mind. Sin seen in the glass of the law is a terrible thing; no man can behold it and live. "When the commandment came, sin revived, and I died;" when it came from God to my conscience, as managed by an almighty arm, then it slew me. And now is the time to confess sin, because now a soul knows what it is, and sees what it is, both in the nature and consequence of it.

2. To a right confession of sin, there must be sound knowledge of God, es-

pecially as to his justice, holiness, righteousness, and purity; wherefore the Publican here begins his confession by calling upon or by the acknowledgement of his Majesty: "God be merciful to me a sinner:" As if he should say, God, O God, O great God, O sin- revenging God, I have sinned against thee, I have broken thy law, I have opposed thy holiness, thy justice, thy law, and thy righteous will. O consuming fire ("for our God is a consuming fire"), I have justly provoked thee to wrath, and to take vengeance on me for my transgressions. But alas! how few that make confession of sin have right apprehension of God, unto whom confession of sin doth belong. Alas! it is easy for men to entertain such apprehensions of God as shall please their own humours, to bear up under the sense of sin, and that shall make their confession rather facile and fantastical, than solid and heartbreaking. The sight and knowledge of the great God is, to sinful man, the most dreadful thing in the world; which makes confession of sin so rare. Most men confess their sins behind God's back, but few to his face; and you know there is ofttimes a vast difference in thus doing among men.

3. To the right confession of sin, there must be a deep conviction of the terribleness of the day of judgment. This John the Baptist inserts, where he insinuates, that the Pharisees' want of (sense of, and) the true confession of sin; was because they had not been warned (or had not taken the alarm) to flee from the wrath to come. What dread, terror, or frightful apprehension can there be, where there is no sense of a day of judgment, and of our giving unto God an account for it? Matth. iii. 7; Luke iii. 7.

I say, therefore, to confession of sin, there must be,

(1.) A deep conviction of the certainty of the day of judgment; namely, that such a day is coming, that such a day shall be. This the apostle insinuates, where he saith, "God commandeth all men, every where, to repent: because he hath appointed a day in the which he will judge the world in righteousness by that man whom he hath ordained, whereof he hath given assurance unto all men, in that he hath raised him from the dead;" Acts xvii. 30, 31.

This will give a sense of what the soul must expect at that day for sin, and so will drive to an hearty acknowledgement of it, and strong cries for a deliverance from it. For thus will the soul argue that expecteth the judgment-day, and that believes that it must count for all. O my heart! it is in vain now to dissemble, or to hide, or to lessen transgressions; for there is a judgment to come, a day in which God will judge the secrets of men by his Son; and at that day he will bring to light the hidden things of darkness, and will manifest the counsels of the heart. If it must be so then, to what end will it be now to seek to dissemble? 1 Cor. iv. 5. This also is in the Old Testament urged as an argument to cause youth, and persons of all sizes, to recall themselves to sobriety, and so to confession of their sin to God; where the Holy Ghost saith ironically, "Rejoice, O young man, in thy youth, and let thy heart cheer thee in the days of thy youth, and walk in the ways of thine heart, and in the sight of thine eyes: but know thou that for all these things God will bring thee into judgment." So again, "God shall bring every work into judgment, with every secret thing, whether it be good or whether it be evil," Eccles. xi. 9; xii. 12, 14.

The certainty of this, I say, must go to the producing of sincere confession of sin; and this is intimated by the Publican, who within his confession, addeth, "God be merciful to me a sinner." As if he should say, If thou art not merciful to me, thy judgment shall swallow me up: without thy mercy I shall not stand, but fall by the judgment which thou hast appointed.

(2.) As there must be, for the producing of sincere confession of sin, a deep conviction of the certainty, so of the terribleness, of the day of judgment: wherefore the apostle, to put men on repentance, which is sincere confession of sin, saith, "For we must all appear before the judgment-seat of Christ, that every one may receive the things done in his body, according to that he hath done, whether it be good or bad. Knowing therefore the terror of the Lord, we persuade men;" 2 Cor. v. 10, 11. The terror of the Lord, as we see here, he makes use of, to persuade men to confession of sin, and repentance to God for mercy.

And I am persuaded, that one reason that this day doth so swarm with wanton professors, is, because they have not sound conviction for, nor go to God with sincere confession of, sin: and one cause of that has been, that they did never seriously fall in with, nor yet sink under either the certainty or terribleness, of the day of judgment.

O the terrors of the Lord! the amazing face that will be put upon all things before the tribunal of God! Yea, the terror that will then be read in the face of God, of Christ, of saints and angels, against the ungodly! Whoso believes and understands it, cannot live without confession of sin to God, and a coming to him for mercy.

"Mountains, fall upon us, and cover us, and hide us from the face of him that sits upon the throne, and from the wrath of the Lamb; for the great day of his wrath is come, and who is able to stand?" This terror is also signified, where it is said, "And I saw a great white throne, and him that sat on it, from whose face the (very) earth and the heaven fled away: and there was found no place for them. And I saw the dead, small and great, stand before God: and the books were opened; and another book was opened, which is the book of life: and the dead were judged out of those things which were written in the books, according to their works. And the sea gave up the dead which were in it; and death and hell delivered up the dead which were in them: and they were judged every man according to his works. And death and hell were cast into the lake of fire. This is the second death. And whosoever was not found written in the book of life, was cast into the lake of fire;" Rev. xx. Here is terror; and this is revealed in the word of God, that sinners might hear and consider it, and so come and confess, and implore God's mercy.

The terror of the Lord, how will it appear, when he "shall be revealed from heaven with his mighty angels, in flaming fire, taking vengeance on them that know not God, and that obey not the gospel of our Lord Jesus Christ!" 2 Thess. i. 7-9.

The terror of the Lord, how will it appear, when his wrath shall burn and flame out like an oven or a fiery furnace before him, while the wicked stand in his sight! Matt. xiii. 50.

The terror of the Lord, how will it appear, while the angels at his command shall gather the wicked to burn them! "As the tares are gathered and burned in the fire, so shall it be in the end of this world. The Son of man shall send forth his angels, and they shall gather together out of his kingdom all things that offend, and them that do iniquity, and shall cast them into a furnace of fire, where there shall be wailing and gnashing of teeth;" Matt. xiii. 40-42. Who can conceive this terror! much more unable are men to express it with tongue or pen; yet the truly penitent and sin-confessing Publican hath apprehension so far thereof, by the word of the testimony, that it driveth him to God with a confession of sin for an interest in God's mercy. But,

4. To right and sincere confession of sin there must be a conviction of a probability of mercy. This also is intimated by the Publican in his confession; "God (saith he) be merciful to me a sinner." He had some glimmerings of mercy, some

conviction of a probability of mercy, or that he might obtain mercy for his pardon, if he went and with unfeigned lips did confess his sins to God.

Despair of mercy shuts up the mouth, makes the heart hard, and drives a man away from God; as is manifest in the case of Adam and the fallen angels. But the least intimation of mercy, if the heart can but touch, feel, taste, or have the least probability of it, that will open the mouth, tend to soften the heart, and to make a very publican come up to God into the temple, and say, "God be merciful to me a sinner."

There must then be this holy mixture of things in the heart of a truly confessing publican. There must be sound sense of sin, sound knowledge of God, deep conviction of the certainty and terribleness of the day of judgment, as also of the probability of obtaining mercy. But to come to that which remains; I told you that there were two things that did make unfeigned confession hard. The first I have touched upon.

Secondly, And now the second follows: and that is, some private leaning to some goodness a man shall conceit that he hath done before, or is doing now, or that he purposeth to prevail with God for the pardon of sins. This man, to be sure, knows not sin in the nature and evil of it, only he has some false apprehensions about it. For where the right knowledge of sin is in the heart, that man sees so much evil in the least transgressions, as that it would break the back of all the angels of heaven should the great God impute it to them. And he that sees this is far enough off from thinking of doing to mitigate or assuage the rigour of the law, or to make pardonable his own transgressions thereby. But he that sees not this, cannot confess his transgressions aright; for true confession consisteth in the general, in a man's taking to himself his transgressions, with the acknowledgment of them to be his, and that he cannot stir from under them, nor do anything to make amends for them, or to palliate the rigour of justice against the soul. And this the Publican did when he cried, "God be merciful to me a sinner."

He made his sins his own; he stood before God in them, accounting that he was surely undone for ever, if God did not extend forgiveness unto him. And this is to do as the prophet Jeremiah bids; to wit, only to acknowledge our iniquities, to acknowledge them at the terrible bar of God's justice, until mercy takes them out of the way; not by doing, or promising to do, either this or that good work. And the reason of this kind of confession is,

(1.) Because this carrieth in it the true nature of confession; to confess, and plead for mercy under the crimes confessed, without shifts and evasions, is the only real simple way of confession. "I said, I will confess my transgressions to the Lord;" and what then? "and thou forgavest the iniquity of my sin." Mark, nothing comes in betwixt confession and forgiveness of sin, Psalm xxxii. 5; nothing of works of righteousness, nothing of legal amendments, nothing but an outcry for mercy; and that act is so far off from lessening the offence, that it greatly heightens and aggravates it. That is the first reason.

(2.) A second reason is, Because God doth expect that the penitent confessors should not only confess, but bear their shame on them: yea, saith God, "Be thou confounded also, and bear thine own shame:" when God takes away thine iniquity, thou shalt "be confounded, and never open thy mouth more, because of thy shame;" Ezek. xvi. 52, 54, 62, 63. We count it convenient that men, when their crimes and transgressions are to be manifested, that they be set in some open place with a piece paper, wherein their transgressions are inserted, that they may not only confess, but bear their own shame. At the penitential confession of sinners God has something to do; if not before men, yet before angels, that they may behold, and be affected, and rejoice when they shall see, after the revelation of sin, the sinner taken into the favour and abundant mercy of God; Luke xv.

(3.) A third reason is, for that God will, in the forgiveness of sin, magnify the riches of his mercy; but this cannot be, if God shall suffer, or accept of such confession of sin, as is yet intermixed with those things that will darken the heinousness of the offence.

That God, in the salvation, and so in the confession, of the sinner, designs the magnifying of his mercy, is apparent enough from the whole current of scripture; and that any of the things now mentioned will, if suffered to be done, darken and eclipse this thing, is evident to reason itself.

Suppose a man stand indicted for treason, yet shall so order the matter that it shall ring in the country that his offences are but petty crimes; though the king shall forgive the man, much glory shall not thereby redound to the riches and greatness of his mercy. But let all things lie naked, let nothing lie hid or covered, let sin be seen, shewn, and confessed, as it is in the sinner himself, and then there will be in his forgiveness a magnifying of mercy.

(4.) A fourth reason is, for else God cannot be justified in his sayings, nor overcome when he is judged; Psalm li.; Rom. iii. God's word hath told us what sin is, both as to its nature and evil effects; God's word hath told us, that the best of our righteousness is no better than filthy rags. God's word has also told us, that sin is forgiven us freely by grace, and not for the sake of our amendments: and all this God shews, not only in the acts of his mercy toward, but even in the humiliations and confessions of, the penitent; for God will have his mercy to be displayed even there where the sinner hath taken his first step toward him: "That as sin hath reigned unto death, even so grace might reign through righteousness unto eternal life by Jesus Christ our Lord;" Rom. v. 21.

(5.) A fifth reason is, because God would have by the Publican's conversion others affected with the displays and discoveries of wonderful grace, but not to cloud and cover it with lessening of sin.

For what will such say when sin begins to appear to conscience, and when the law shall follow it with a voice of words, each one like a clap of thunder? I say, what will such say, when they shall read that the Publican did only acknowledge his iniquity, and found grace and favour of God? That God is infinitely merciful to those or to such as in truth stand in need of mercy. Also, that he sheweth mercy of his own good pleasure, nothing moving him thereto.

I say, this is the way to make others be affected with mercy, as he saith, by the apostle Paul, "But God, who is rich in mercy, for his great love wherewith he loved us, even when we were dead in sins, hath quickened us together with Christ (by grace ye are saved); and hath raised us up together, and made us sit together in heavenly places in Christ Jesus; that in the ages to come he might shew the exceeding riches of his grace in his kindness to us-ward (or toward us) through Christ Jesus;" Eph. ii. 4-7. You may also see that 1 Tim. i. 15, 16.

(6.) Another reason of this is, because this is the way to heighten the comfort and consolation of the soul, and that both here and hereafter. What tendeth more to this, than for sinners to see, and with guilt and amazement to confess, what sin is, and so to have pardon extended from God to the sinner as such? This fills the heart; it ravishes the soul; puts joy into the thoughts of salvation from sin, and deliverance from wrath to come. Now they "return, and comb to Zion with songs, and everlasting joy upon their heads: they shall obtain joy and gladness, and sorrow and sighing shall flee away;" Isa. xxxv. 10. Indeed, the belief of this makes joy and gladness endless.

(7.) Besides, it layeth upon the soul the greatest obligations to holiness. What like the apprehension of free forgiveness (and that apprehension must come in through a sight of the greatness of sin, and of inability to do any thing towards satisfaction), to engage the heart of a rebel to love his prince, and to submit to his laws?

When Elisha had taken the Syrian captives, some were for using severities towards them; but he said, "Set bread and water before them, that they may eat and drink and go to their master;" and they did so. And what follows? "So the bands of Syria came no more into the land of Israel,"--he conquered their malice with his compassion. And it is the love of Christ that constraineth to live to him; 2 Kings vi. 13-23; 2 Cor. v. 14.

Many other things might possibly be urged, but at present let these be sufficient.

The SECOND thing that we made mention of in the Publican's prayer, was an imploring of help against this malady: "God be merciful to me a sinner." In which petition I shall take notice of several things.

First, That a man's help against sin doth not so absolutely lie in his personal conquest as in the pardon of them. I suppose a conquest, though there can indeed by man be none so long as he liveth in this world, I mean, a complete conquest and annihilation of sin.

The Publican, and so every graciously awakened sinner, is doubtless for the subduing of sin; but yet he looketh that the chief help against it doth lie in the pardon of it. Suppose a man should stab his neighbour with his knife, and afterwards burn his knife to nothing in the fire, would this give him help against his murder? No, verily, nothwithstanding this, his neck is obnoxious to the halter, yea, and his soul to hell-fire. But a pardon gives him absolute help: It is God that justifies; who shall condemn? Rom. viii. Suppose a man should live many days in rebellion against God, and after that leave off to live any longer so rebelliously, would this help him against the guilt which he had contracted before? No, verily; without remission there is no help, but the rebel is undone. Wherefore the first blessedness, yea, and that without which all other things cannot make one blessed, it lies in pardon. "Blessed is he whose transgression is forgiven, whose sin is covered. Blessed is the man unto whom the Lord will not impute sin;" Psalm xxxii.; Rom. iv.

Suppose a man greatly sanctified and made holy; I say, suppose it: yet if the sins before committed by him be not pardoned, he cannot be a blessed man.

Yet again, suppose a man should be caught up to heaven, not having his sins pardoned; heaven itself cannot make him a blessed man. I suppose these things-- not that they can be--to illustrate my matter. There can be no blessedness upon any man who yet remaineth unforgiven. You see therefore here, that there was much of the wisdom of the Holy Ghost in this prayer of the Publican. He was directed the right, the only, the next way to shelter, where blessedness begins, even to mercy for the pardon of his sins. Alas! what would it advantage a traitor to be taken up into the king's coach, to be clothed with the king's royal robe, to have put upon his finger the king's gold ring, and to be made to wear, for the present, a chain of gold about his neck, if after all this the king should say unto him, But I will not pardon thy rebellion; thou shalt die for thy treason? Pardon, then, to him that loves life, is better, and more to be preferred and sought after, than all other things; yea, it is the highest wisdom in any sinner to seek after that first.

This therefore confuteth the blindness of some, and the hypocrisy of others. Some are so silly and so blind as quite to forget and look over the pardon of sin, and to lay their happiness in some external amendments, when, alas! poor wretches as they are, they abide under the wrath of God. Or if they be not quite so foolish as utterly to forget the forgiveness of sin, yet they think of it but in the second place; they are for setting of sanctification before justification, and so seek to confound the order of God; and that which is worse unto them, they by so doing do what they can to keep themselves indeed from being sharers in that great blessing of forgiveness of sins by grace.

But the Publican here was guided by the wisdom of heaven. He comes into the temple, he confesseth himself a sinner, and forthwith, without any delay, before he removeth his foot from where he stands, craves help of pardon; for he knew that all other things, if he remained in guilt, would not help him against that damnation that belonged to a vile and unforgiven sinner.

This also confuteth the hypocrites, such as is our Pharisee here in the text, that glory in nothing so much as that they are not as other men, not unjust, no adulterer, no extortioner, nor even as this Publican; and thus miss of the forgiveness of sin; and if they have missed of the beginning good, they shall never, as so standing, receive the second or the third. Justification, sanctification, glorification, they are the three things, but the order of God must not be perverted. Justification must be first, because that comes to man while he is ungodly and a sinner.

Justification cannot be where God has not passed a pardon. A pardon, then, is the first thing to be looked after by the sinner. This the Pharisee did not; therefore he went down to his house unjustified; he set the stumbling-block of his iniquity before his face when he went to inquire of the Lord; and as he neglected, slighted, scorned, because he thought that he had no need of pardon, therefore it was given to the poor, needy, and miserable Publican, and he went away with the blessing.

Publicans, since this is so weighty a point, let me exhort you that you do not forget this prayer of your wise and elder brother, to wit, the Publican that went up into the temple to pray. I say, forget it not, neither suffer any vain-glorious or self-conceited hypocrites with argument to allure you with their silly and deceitful tongues from this wholesome doctrine. Remember that you are sinners as abominable as the Publican, wherefore do you, as you have him for your pattern, go to God, confess, in all simple, honest, and self- abasing, your numerous and abominable sins; and be sure that in the very next place you forget not to ask for pardon, saying, "God be merciful to me a sinner." And remember that none but God can help you against, nor keep you from, the damnation and misery that comes by sin.

Secondly, As the Publican imploreth help, so notwithstanding the sentence of the law that is gone out against him, he saith to God, Be merciful to me: and also in that he concludes himself a sinner. I say, he justifieth, he approveth of the sentence of the law, that was now gone out against him, and by which he now stood condemned in his own conscience before the tribunal of God's justice. He saith not as the hypocrite, Because I am innocent, surely his anger shall turn from me; or, What have we spoken so much against thee? No, he is none of these murmurs or complainers, but fairly falls before the law, witnesses, judge, and jury, and consenteth to the verdict, sentence, and testimony of each of them; Jer. ii. 36; Mal. ii. 13.

To illustrate this a little, suppose a malefactor should be arraigned before a judge, and that after the witnesses, jury, and judge, have all condemned him to death for his fact, the judge again should ask, him what he can say for himself why sentence of death should not pass upon him? Now, if he saith, Nothing, but good my lord, mercy; he confesseth the indictment, approveth of the verdict of the jury, and consenteth to the judgment of the judge.

The Publican therefore in crying, Mercy, justifieth the sentence of the law that was gone out against his sins. He wrangleth not with the law, saying, that was too severe; though many men do thus, saying, "God forbid; for then woe be to us." He wrangleth not with the witness, which was his own conscience; though some will buffet, smite, and stop its mouth, or command it to be silent. He wrangleth not with the jury, which were the prophets and apostles; though some men cannot abide to hear all that they say. He wrangleth not with the judge, nor sheweth himself irreverently before him; but in all humble gestures that could bespeak him acquiescing with the sentence, he flieth to mercy for relief.

Nor is this alone the way of the Publican; but of other godly men before his time. When David was condemned, he justified the sentence and the judge, out of whose mouth it proceeded, and so fled for succour to the mercy of God; Psalm li. When Shemaiah the prophet pronounced God's judgments against the princes of Judah for their sin, they said, "The Lord is righteous." When the church in the Lamentations had reckoned up several of her grievous afflictions wherewith she had been chastised, she, instead of complaining, doth justify the Lord, and approve of the sentence that was passed upon her, saying, "The Lord is righteous; for I have rebelled against his commandment." So Daniel, after he had enumerated the evils that befel the church in his day, addeth, "Therefore hath the Lord brought it upon us; for the Lord our God is righteous in all his works which he doth: for we obeyed not his voice;" 2 Chron. xii. 6, Lam. i. 18; Dan. ix. 14.

And this is the case with our Publican. He has transgressed a law that is holy, just, and good: the witness that accuseth him of this is God and his conscience; he is also cast by the verdict of holy men; and all this he knows, and implicitly confesses, even in that he directs his prayer unto his judge for pardon. And it is one of the excellentest sights in the world, to see or understand a sinner thus honestly receiving the sentence of the law that is gone out against him; to see and hear a Publican thus to justify God. And this God would have men do for these reasons.

1. That it might be conspicuous to all that the Publican has need of mercy. This

is for the glory of the justice of God, because it vindicates it in its goings out against the Publican. God loveth to do things in justice and righteousness, when he goeth out against men, though it be but such a going out against them as only tendeth to their conviction and conversion. When he dealt with our father Abraham in this matter, he called him to his foot, as here he doth the Publican. And, sinner, if God counts thee worthy to inherit the throne of glory, he will bring thee hither. But,

2. The Publican, by the power of conviction, stoops to, and falleth under, the righteous sentence gone forth against him, that it might be also manifest, that what afterward he shall receive is of the mere grace and sovereign goodness of God. And indeed there is no way that doth more naturally tend to make this manifest than this. For thus; there is a man proceeded against for life by the law, and the sentence of death is, in conclusion, most justly and righteously passed upon him by the judge. Suppose now, that after this, this man lives, and is exalted to honour, enjoys great things, and is put into place of trust and power, and that by him that he has offended, even by him that did pass the sentence upon him.

What will all say, or what will they conclude, even upon the very first hearing of this story? Will they not say,--Well, whoever he was that found himself wrapped up in this strange providence, must thank the mercy of a gracious prince; for all these things bespeak grace and favour. But,

3. As the Publican falleth willingly under the sentence, and justifieth the passing of it upon him; so by his flying to mercy for help, he declareth to all that he cannot deliver himself: he putteth help away from himself, or saith, It is not in me.

This, I say, is another thing included in this prayer, and it is a thing distinct from that. For it is possible for a man to justify, and fall under, the sentence of the judge, and yet retain that with himself that will certainly deliver him from that sentence when it has done its worst. Many have held up their hand, and cried Guilty, at the bar, and yet have fetched themselves off for all that; but then they have not pleaded mercy (for he that doth so, puts his life altogether into the hands of another), but privilege or good deeds, either done or to be done by them. But the Publican in our text puts all out of his own hand; and in effect saith to that God before whom he went up into the temple to pray, Lord, I stand here condemned at the bar of thy justice, and that worthily, for the sentence is good, and hath in righteousness gone out against me: nor can I deliver myself: I heartily and freely confess I cannot; wherefore I betake myself only to thy mercy, and do pray thee to forgive the transgressions of me a sinner. O how few be there of such kind of publicans, I mean of publicans thus made sensible, that come unto God for mercy!

Mercy, with most, is rather a compliment, I mean while they plead it with God, than a matter of absolute necessity; they have not awfully, and in judgment and conscience, fallen under the sentence, nor put themselves out of all plea but the plea of mercy; indeed, thus to do is the effect of the proof of the vanity and emptiness of all experiments made use of before.

Now, there is a twofold proof of experiments; the one is the result of practice, the other is the result of faith.

The woman with her bloody issue made her proof by practice, when she had spent all that she had upon physicians, and was nothing bettered, but rather grew worse; Mark v. But our Publican here proves the emptiness and vanity of any other helps, by one cast of faith upon the contents of the Bible, and by another look upon his present state of condemnation; wherefore he presently, without any more ado, condemneth all other helps, ways, modes, or means of deliverance, and betakes himself only to the mercy of God: saying, "God be merciful to me a sinner."

And herein he sheweth wonderful wisdom. For,

1. By this he thrusts himself under the shelter and blessing of the promise; and I am sure it is better and safer to do so, than to rely upon the best of excellencies that this world can afford: Hos. xiv. 1-3.

2. He takes the ready way to please God: for God takes more delight in shewing of mercy than in any thing that we can do; Hos. vi. 6; Matt. ix. 13; xii. 7. Yea, and that also is the man that pleaseth him, even he that hopes in his mercy; Psalm cxlvii. 11. The Publican, therefore, whatever the Pharisee might think, stood all this while upon sure ground, and had by far the start of him for heaven. Alas! his dull head could look no further than to the conceit of the pitiful beauty and splendour of his own filthy righteousness. Nor durst he leave that to trust wholly to the mercy of God; but the Publican comes out, though in his sins, yet like an awakened, enlightened, resolved man, and first abases himself, then gives God the glory of his justice, and after that the glory of his mercy, by saying, "God be merciful to me a sinner;" and thus in the ears of the angels he did ring the changes of heaven. And,

3. The Publican, in his thus putting himself upon mercy, sheweth, that in his

opinion there is more virtue in mercy to save, than there is in the law and sin to condemn. And although this is not counted a great matter to do, while men are far from the law, and while their conscience is asleep within them; yet when the law comes near, and conscience is awake, who so tries it will find it a laborious work. Cain could not do thus for his heart, no, nor Saul; nor Judas either. This is another kind of thing than most men think it to be, or shall find it, whenever they shall behold God's angry face, and when they shall hear the words of his law.

However, our Publican did it, and ventured his body, soul, and future condition for ever on this bottom with other the saints and servants of God, leaving the world to swim over the sea of God's wrath (if they will) in their weak and simple vessels of bulrushes, or to lean upon their cobweb-hold, when he shall arise to the judgment that he hath appointed.

In the mean time, pray God awaken us as he did the Publican; pray God enlighten us as he did the Publican; pray God grant us boldness to come to him as the Publican did; and also in that trembling spirit as he did, when he cried in the temple before him, "God be merciful to me a sinner."

Thus having passed over his prayer, we come in the next place to his GESTURES; for in my judgment the right understanding of them will give us yet more conviction of the Publican's sense and awakening of spirit under this present action of his.

And I have observed many a poor wretch that hath readily had recourse to the Publican's prayer, that never knew what the Publican's gestures, in the presence of God, while in prayer before him, did mean. Nor must any man be admitted to think, that those gestures of his were a custom, and a formality among the Jews in those days; for it is evident enough by the carriage of the Pharisee, that it was below them and their mode, when they came into the temple, or when they prayed any where else; and they in those days were counted for the best of men; and in religious matters men were to imitate and take their examples at the hands of the best, not at the hands of the worst.

The Publican's gestures then were properly his own; caused by the guilt of sin, and by that dread of the majesty of God that was upon his spirit. And a comely posture it was, else Christ Jesus, the Son of God, would never have taken that particular notice thereof as he did, nor have smiled upon it so much as to take, and distinctly repeat it, as that which made his prayer the more weighty, also to be taken notice of. Yea, in my opinion, the Lord Jesus committed it to record, for that he liked it, and for that it will pass for some kind of touchstone of prayer that is made in good sense of sin and of God, and of need of his goodness and mercy. For verily, all these postures signify sense, sight of a lost condition, and a heart in good earnest for mercy.

I know that they may be counterfeited, and Christ Jesus knows who doth so too; but that will not hinder, or make weak or invalid what hath already been spoken about it. But to forbear to make a further prologue, and to come to the handling of particulars:

"And the Publican standing afar off, would not lift up so much as his eyes to heaven, but smote upon his breast," &c.

Three things, as I told you already, we may perceive in these words, by which his publican posture or gestures are set forth.

1. He stands "afar off."
2. He "would not lift up so much as his eyes to heaven."
3. He "smote upon his breast," &c.

For the first of these, He stood afar off. "And the Publican standing afar off." This is, I say, the first thing, the first posture of his with which we are acquainted, and it informeth us of several things.

First, That he came not with senselessness of the majesty of God when he came to pray, as the Pharisee did, and as sinners commonly do. For this standing back, or afar off, declares, that the majesty of God had an awe upon his spirit; he saw whither, to whom, and for what, he was now approaching the temple. It is said in the 20th of Exodus, that when the people saw the thunderings and lightnings, and the noise of the trumpet, and the mountain smoking (and all these were signs of God's terrible presence and dreadful majesty), they removed themselves, and "stood afar off;" Exod. xx. 18. This behaviour, therefore, of the Publican did well become his present action, especially since, in his own eyes, he was yet an unforgiven sinner. Alas! what is God's majesty to a sinful man but a consuming fire? And what is a sinful man in himself, or in his approach to God, but as stubble fully dry?

How then could the Publican do otherwise (than what he did) than stand afar off if he either thought of God or himself? Indeed the people afore named, before they saw God in his terrible majesty, could scarcely be kept off from the mount with words and bounds, as it is now the case of many: their blindness gives them boldness; their rudeness gives them confidence; but when they shall see what the Publican saw, and felt, and understood, as he, they will pray and stand afar off even as these people did. They removed and stood afar off, and then fell to praying of Moses, that this dreadful sight and sound might be taken from them. And what if I should say, he stood afar off for fear of a blow, though he came for mercy, as it is said of them, "They stood afar off for fear of her torments;" Rev. xviii. 10, 18.

I know what it is to go to God for mercy, and stand all that while through fear afar off; being possessed with this, will not God now smite me at once to the ground for my sins? David thought something when he said as he prayed, "Cast me not away from thy presence; and take not thy Holy Spirit from me;" Psalm li. 11.

There is none knows, but those that have them, what turns and returns, what coming on and going off, there is in the spirit of a man that indeed is awakened, and that stands awakened before the glorious Majesty in prayer. The prodigal also made his prayer to his Father intentionally, while he was yet a great way off. And so did the lepers too: "And as he entered into a certain village there met him ten men that were lepers, which stood afar off: and they lifted up their voices and said, Jesus, Master, have mercy on us;" Luke xvii. 12, 13.

See here, it has been the custom of praying men to keep their distance, and not to be rudely bold in rushing into the presence of the holy and heavenly Majesty, especially if they have been sensible of their own vileness and sins, as the prodigal, the lepers, and our poor Publican was. Yea, Peter himself, when upon a time he perceived more than commonly he did of the majesty of Jesus his Lord, what doth he do? "When Simon Peter saw it (says the text), he fell down at Jesus' knees, saying, Depart from me, for I am a sinful man, O Lord;" Luke v. 3-8. Oh! when men see God and themselves, it fills them with holy fear of the greatness of the majesty of God, as well as with love to, and desire after, his mercy.

Besides, by his standing afar off, it might be to intimate that he now had in mind, and with great weight upon his conscience, the infinite distance that was betwixt God and him. Men should know that, and tremble in the thoughts of it, when they are about to approach the omnipotent presence.

What is poor sorry man, poor dust and ashes, that he should crowd it up, and go jostlingly into the presence of the great God--especially since it is apparent the disproportion that is betwixt God and him? Esther, when she went to supplicate the king her husband for her people, made use neither of her beauty nor relation, nor the privileges of which she might have had temptation to make use of, especially at such a time, and in such exigencies, as then did compass her about; but, I say, she made not use of them to thrust herself into his presence, but knew, and kept her distance, standing in the inward court of his palace until he held out the golden sceptre to her; then Esther drew near, and touched the top thereof; Esth. v. 1, 2.

Men, also, when they come into the presence of God, should know their distance; yea, and shew that they know it too, by such gestures, and carriages, and behaviour, that are seemly. A remarkable saying is that of Solomon, "Keep thy foot," saith he, "when thou goest into the house of God, and be more ready to hear than to give the sacrifice of fools; for they consider not that they do evil." And as they should keep their foot, so also he adds, "Be not rash with thy mouth, and let not thine heart be hasty to utter any thing before God; for God is in heaven, and thou upon earth, therefore let thy words be few;" Eccles. v. 1, 2.

Three things the Holy Ghost exhorteth to in this text.

The one is, That we look to our feet, and not be forward to crowd into God's presence.

Another is, That we should also look well to our tongues, that they be not rash in uttering any thing before God.

And the third is, Because of the infinite distance that is betwixt God and us, which is intimated by these words, "For God is in heaven, and thou upon earth."

The Publican therefore shewed great wisdom, holy shame, and humility, in this brave gesture of his, namely, in his standing afar off when he went up into the temple to pray. But this is not all.

Secondly, The Publican, in standing afar off, left room for an Advocate and high-priest, a Day's-man, to come betwixt, to make peace between God and his poor creature. Moses, the great mediator of the Old Testament, was to go nigher to God than the rest of the elders, or those of the people; Exod. xx. 21. Yea, the rest of the people were expressly commanded to worship, "standing afar off." No man of the sons of Aaron that had a blemish was to come nigh. "No man that hath a blemish of the seed of Aaron the priest shall come nigh to offer the offerings of the Lord made by fire. He shall not come nigh to offer the bread of his God;" Lev. xxi. 21.

The Publican durst not be his own mediator; he knew he had a blemish, and was infirm, and therefore he stands back; for he knew that it was none of him that his God had chosen to come near unto him, to offer "the fat and the blood;" Ezek. xliv. 13-15. The Publican, therefore, was thus far right; he took not up the room himself, neither with his person nor his performances, but stood back, and gave place to the High-priest that was to be intercessor.

We read, that when Zacharias went into the temple to burn incense, as at the time his lot was, "The whole multitude of the people were praying without;" Luke i. 9, 10. They left him where he was, near to God, between God and them, mediating for them; for the offering of incense by the chief-priest was a figurative making of intercession for the people, and they maintained their distance.

It is a great matter in praying to God, not to go too far, nor come too short, in that duty, I mean in the duty of prayer; and a man is very apt to do one or the other. The Pharisee went so far; he was too bold; he came into the temple making such a ruffle with his own excellencies, that there was in his thoughts no need of a Mediator. He also went up so nigh to God, that he took up the room and place of the Mediator himself; but this poor Publican, he knows his distance, and keeps it, and leaves room for the High-priest to come and intercede for him with God. He stood afar off: not too far off; for that is the room and place of unbelievers; and in that sense this saying is true, "For, lo, they that are far from thee shall perish;" Psalm lxxiii. 27; that is, they whose unbelief hath set their hearts and affections more upon their idols, and that have been made to cast God behind their backs, to follow and go a-whoring after them.

Hitherto, therefore, it appears, that though the Pharisee had more righteousness than the Publican, yet the Publican had more spiritual righteousness than the Pharisee; and that though the Publican had a baser and more ugly outside than the Pharisee, yet the Publican knew how to prevail with God for mercy better than he.

As for the Publican's posture of standing in prayer, it is excusable, and that by the very Father of the faithful himself: for Abraham stood praying when he made intercession for Sodom; Gen. xviii. 22, 23. Christ also alloweth it, where he saith, "And when ye stand praying, forgive, if ye have ought against any; that your Father also which is in heaven may forgive you your trespasses;" Mark xi. 25. Indeed there is no stinted order prescribed for our thus behaving of ourselves in prayer, whether kneeling, or standing, or walking, or lying, or sitting; for all these postures have been used by the godly. Paul "kneeled down and prayed;" Acts xx. 36. Abraham and the Publican stood and prayed. David prayed as he walked; 2 Sam. xv. 30, 31. Abraham prayed lying upon his face; Gen. xvii. 17,18. Moses prayed sitting; Exod. xvii. 12. And indeed prayer, effectual fervent prayer, may be, and often is, made unto God under all these circumstances of behaviour: for God has not tied us up to any of them; and he that shall tie himself, or his people, to any of these, doth more than he hath warrant for from God: and let such take care of innovating; it is the next way to make men hypocrites and dissemblers in those duties in which they should be sincere.

True, which of those soever a man shall choose to himself for the present, to perform this solemn duty in, it is required of him, and God expects it, that he should pray to him in truth, and with desire, affection, and hunger, after those things that with his tongue he maketh mention of before the throne of God. And indeed without this, all is nothing. But alas! how few be there in the world whose heart and mouth in prayer shall go together? Dost thou, when thou askest for the Spirit, or faith, or love to God, to holiness, to saints, to the word, and the like, ask for them with love to them, desire of them, hungering after them? Oh! this is a mighty thing! and yet prayer is no more before God, than as it is seasoned with these blessed qualifications. Wherefore it is said, that while men are praying, God is searching of the heart, to see what is the meaning of the Spirit (or whether there be the Spirit and his meaning in all that the mouth hath uttered, either by words, sighs, or groans), because it is by him, and through his help only, that any make prayers according to the will of God; Rom. viii. 26, 27. Whatever thy posture therefore shall be, see that thy prayers be pertinent and fervent, not mocking of thine own soul with words, while thou wantest, and art an utter stranger to, the very vital and living spirit of prayer.

Now, our Publican had and did exercise the very spirit of prayer in prayer. He prayed sensibly, seriously, affectionately, hungering, thirsting, and with longing after that for which with his mouth he implored the God of heaven; his heart and soul was in his words, and it was that which made his prayer PRAYER; even because he prayed in PRAYER; he prayed inwardly as well as outwardly.

David tells us, that God heard the voice of his supplication, the voice of his cry, the voice of his tears, and the voice of his roaring. For indeed are all these acceptable. Affection and fervent desire make them sound well in the ears of God. Tears, supplications, prayers, cries, may be all of them done in formality, hypocrisy, and from other causes, and to other ends, than that which is honest and right in God's sight: for God would search and look after the voice of his tears, supplications, roarings, prayers, and cries.

And if men had less care to please men, and more to please God, in the matter and manner of praying, the world would be at a better pass than it is. But this is not in man's power to help and to amend. When the Holy Ghost comes upon men with great conviction of their state and condition, and of the use and excellency of the grace of sincerity and humility in prayer, then, and not till then, will the grace of prayer be more prized, and the specious, flounting, complimentary lips of flatterers, be more laid aside. I have said it already, and will say it again, that there is now-a-days a great deal of wickedness committed in the very duty of prayer; by words of which men have no sense by reaching after such conclusion and clenshes therein, as make their persons be admired; by studying for, and labouring after, such enlargements as the spirit accompanieth not the heart in. O Lord God, make our hearts upright in us, as in all points and parts of our profession, so in this solemn appointment of God! "If I regard iniquity in my heart," said David, "the Lord will not hear my prayer." But if I be truly sincere, he will; and then it is no matter whether I kneel, or stand, or sit, or lie, or walk; for I shall do none of these, nor put up my prayers under any of these circumstances, lightly, foolishly, and idly, but to beautify this gesture with the inward working of my mind and spirit in prayer; that whether I stand or sit, walk or lie down, grace and gravity, humility and sincerity, shall make my prayer profitable, and my outward behaviour comely in his eyes, with whom (in prayer) I now have to do.

And had not our Publican been inwardly seasoned with these, Christ would have taken but little pleasure in his modes and outward behaviour: but being so honest inwardly, and in the matter of his prayer, his gestures by that were made beauteous also; and therefore it is that our Lord so delightfully delateth upon them, and draweth them out at length before the eyes of others.

I have often observed, that which is natural and so comely in one, looks odiously when imitated by another. I speak as to gestures and actions in preaching and prayer. Many, I doubt not, but will imitate the Publican, and that both in the prayer and gestures of the Publican, whose persons and actions will yet stink in the nostrils of him that is holy and just, and that searcheth the heart and the reins.

Well, the Publican stood and prayed; he stood afar off, and prayed, and his prayers came even to the ears of God.

"And the Publican standing afar off would not lift up so much as his eyes to heaven," &c.

We are now come to another of his postures. He would not, says the text, so much as lift up his eyes to heaven. Here, therefore, was another gesture added to that which went before; and a gesture that a great while before had been condemned by the Holy Ghost himself. "Is it such a fast that I have chosen, a day for a man to afflict his soul? Is it to bow down his head as a bulrush?" Isa. lviii. 5.

But why condemned then, and smiled upon now? Why? Because done in hypocrisy then, and in sincerity now. Hypocrisy, and a spirit of error, that he shall take no pleasure in them; but sincerity, and honesty in duties, will make even them comely in the sight of men-- may I not say before God? The Rechabites were not commanded of God, but of their father, to do as they did; but, because they were sincere in their obedience thereto, even God himself maketh use of what they did, to condemn the disobedience of the Jews; and, moreover, doth tell the Rechabites at last, that they should not want a man to stand before him for ever. "And Jeremiah said unto the house of the Rechabites, Thus saith the Lord of Hosts, the God of Israel, because ye have obeyed the commandment of Jonadab your father, and kept all his precepts, and done according unto all that he hath commanded you; therefore, thus saith the Lord of Hosts, the God of Israel, Jonadab, the son of Rechab, shall not want a man to stand before me for ever."

He would not lift up his eyes to heaven. Why? Surely because shame had covered his face. Shame will make a man blush and hang his head like a bulrush; shame for sin is a virtue, a comely thing; yea, a beauty-spot in the face of a sinner that cometh to God for mercy.

God complains of the house of Israel, that they could sin, and that without shame; yea, and threateneth them too with sore repeated judgments, because they were not ashamed; it is in Jer. viii. Their crimes in general were, they turned every one to his course, as the horse runneth into the battle. In particular, they were such as rejected God's word; they loved this world, and set themselves against the prophets, crying, "Peace, peace," when they cried, "Judgment, judgment!" And were not ashamed when they had committed abomination; "Nay, they were not at all ashamed, neither could they blush; therefore shall they fall among them that fall: in the time of their visitation they shall be cast down, saith the Lord;" ver. 12. Oh! to stand, or sit, or lie, or kneel, or walk before God in prayer, with blushing cheeks for sin, is one of the most excellent sights that can be seen in the world.

Wherefore the church taketh some kind of heart to herself in that she could lie down in her shame; yea, and makes that a kind of an argument with God to prove that her prayers did come from her heart, and also that he would hear them; Jer. iii. 22-25.

Shame for sin argueth sense of sin, yea, a right sense of sin, a godly sense of sin. Ephraim pleads this when under the hand of God: I was (saith he) "ashamed, yea, even confounded, because I did bear the reproach of my youth." But what follows? "Is Ephraim my dear son? is he a pleasant child? for since I spake against him, I do earnestly remember him still: therefore my bowels are troubled for him: I will surely have mercy upon him, saith the Lord;" Jer. xxxi. 19, 20.

I know that there is a shame that is not the spirit of an honest heart, but that rather floweth from sudden surprisal, when the sinner is unawares taken in the act--in the very manner. And thus sometimes the house of Israel were taken: and then, when they blushed, their shame is compared to the shame of a thief. "As the thief is ashamed when he is found, so is the house of Israel ashamed; they, their kings, their princes, and their priests, and their prophets."

But where were they taken, or about what were they found? Why, they were found "saying to a stock, Thou art my father, and to a stone, thou hast brought me forth." God catched them thus doing; and this made them ashamed, even as the thief is ashamed when the owner doth catch him stealing his horse.

But this was not the Publican's shame. This shame brings not a man into the temple to pray, to stand willingly, and to take shame before God in prayer. This shame makes one rather to fly from his face, and to count one's self most at ease when farthest off from God; Jer. ii. 26, 27.

The Publican's shame, therefore, which he demonstrated by hanging down his head, was godly and holy, and much like that of the prodigal, when he said, "Father, I have sinned against heaven, and in thy sight, and am no more worthy to be called thy son;" Luke xv. 21. I suppose that his postures were much the same with the Publican's, as were his prayers, for the substance of them. O however grace did work in both to the same end! they were both of them, after a godly manner, ashamed of their sins.

"He would not lift up so much as his eyes to heaven."

He could not, he would not: which yet more fully makes it appear, that it was shame, not guilt only, or chiefly, though it is manifest enough that he had guilt; by his crying, "God be merciful to me a sinner." I say, guilt was not the chief cause of hanging down his head, because it saith, he WOULD not; for when guilt is the cause of stooping, it lieth not in the will, or in the power thereof, to help one up.

David tells us, that when he was under guilt, his iniquities were gone over his head: as an heavy burden, they were too heavy for him; and that with them he was bowed down greatly. Or, as he says in another place, "Mine iniquities have taken hold upon me, so that I am not able to look up;" Psalm xxxviii.; xl. I am not able to do it: guilt disableth the understanding, and conscience; shame makes all willingly fall at the feet of Christ.

He would not. He knew what he was, what he had been, and should be, if God had not mercy upon him; yea, he knew also that God knew what he was, had been, and would be, if mercy prevented not; wherefore, thought he, Wherefore should I lift up the head? I am no righteous man, no godly man, I have not served God, but Satan; this I know, this God knows, this angels know, wherefore I will not lift up the head. It is as much as to say, I will not be an hypocrite, like the Pharisee: for lifting up of the head signifies innocency and harmlessness of life, or good conscience, and the testimony thereof, under and in the midst of all accusations. Wherefore this was the counsel of Zophar to Job--"If," saith he, "thou prepare thine heart, and stretch out thine hand towards him; if iniquity be in thine hand, put it far away, and let not wickedness dwell in thy tabernacles. For then shalt thou lift up thy face without spot; yea, thou shalt be steadfast, and shalt not fear;" Job xi. 13-15.

This was not the Publican's state: he had lived in lewdness and villany all his days; nor had he prepared his heart to seek the Lord God of his fathers; he had not cleansed his heart nor hands from violence, nor done that which was lawful and right. He only had been convinced of his evil ways, and was come into the temple as he was, all foul, and in his filthy garments, and amidst his pollutions; how then could he be innocent, holy, or without spot? and, consequently, how could he lift up his face to God? I remember what Abner said to Asahel, "Turn thee aside (said he) from following me, wherefore should I smite thee to the ground? how then should I hold up my face to Joab, thy brother?" 2 Sam. ii. 22.

As if he had said, If I kill thee, I shall blush, be ashamed, and hang my head like a bulrush the next time I come into the company of thy brother.

This was the Publican's case: he was guilty, he had sinned, he had committed a trespass; and now being come into the temple, into the presence of that God whose laws he had broken, and against whom he had sinned, how could he lift up his head? how could he do it? No, it better became him to take his shame, and to hang his head in token of guilt; and indeed he did, and did it to purpose too, for he would not lift up, no not so much as his eyes to heaven.

True, some would have done it; the Pharisee did it; though if he had considered that hypocrisy and the leaning to his own righteousness had been a sin, he would have found as little cause to have done it as did the Publican himself. But, I say he did it, and sped therein; he went down to his house, as he came up into the temple, a poor unjustified Pharisee, whose person and prayer were both rejected; because, like the whore of whom we read in the Proverbs, after he had practised all manner of hypocrisy, he comes into the temple and wipes his mouth, and saith, "I have done no wickedness;" Prov. xxx. 20. He lifts up his head, his face, his eyes, to heaven; he struts, he vaunts himself; he swaggers, he vapours, and cries up himself, saying, "God I thank thee that I am not as other men are."

True, had he come and stood before a stock or stone, he might have said thus, and not have been reprehended; for such are gods that see not, nor hear, neither do they understand. But to come before the true God, the living God, the God that fills heaven and earth by his presence, and that knows the things that come into the mind of man, even every one of them; I say, to come into his house, to stand before him, and thus to lift up his head and eyes in such hypocrisy before him, this was abominable, this was to tempt God, and to prove him, yea, to challenge him to know what was in man, if he could, even as those who said, "How doth God (see) know? can he judge through the dark cloud?" Job xxii. 13; Psalm lxxiii. 11.

But the Publican--no--he would not do this; he would not lift up so much as his eyes to heaven. As who should say, O Lord, I have been against thee a traitor and a rebel, and like a traitor and a rebel before thee will I stand. I will bear my shame before thee in the presence of the holy angels; yea, I will prevent thy judging of me by judging myself in thy sight, and will stand as condemned before thee before thou passest sentence upon me.

This is now for a sinner to go to the end of things. For what is God's design in the work of conviction for sin, and in his awakening of the conscience about it? What is his end, I say, but to make the sinner sensible of what he hath done, and that he might unfeignedly judge himself for the same. Now this our Publican doth; his will therefore is now subjected to the word of God, and he justifies him in all his ways and works towards him. Blessed be God for any experience of these things.

"He would not lift up so much as his eyes to heaven." He knew by his deeds and deservings that he had no portion there; nor would he divert his mind from the remembering, and from being affected with the evil of his ways.

Some men, when they are under the guilt and conviction of their evil life, will do what they can to look any way, and that on purpose to divert their minds, and to call them off from thinking on what they have done; and by their thus doing, they bring many evils more upon their souls; for this is a kind of striving with God, and a shewing a dislike to his ways. Would not you think, if when you are shewing your son or your servant his faults, if he should do what he could to divert and take off his mind from what you are saying, that he striveth against you, and sheweth dislike of your doings? What else mean the complaints of masters and of fathers in this matter? "I have a servant, I have a son, that doth contrary to my will." "O but why do you not chide them for it?" The answer is, "So I do; but they do not regard my words; they do what they can, even while I am speaking, to divert their minds from my words and counsels." Why, all men will cry out, "This is base; this is worthy of great rebuke; such a son, such a servant, deserveth to be shut out of doors, and so made to learn better breeding by want and hardship."

But the Publican would not divert his mind from what at present God was about to make him sensible of, no, not by a look on the choicest object; he would not lift up so much as his eyes to heaven. They are but bad scholars whose eyes, when their master is teaching of them, are wandering off their books.

God saith unto men, when he is teaching them to know the evil of their ways, as the angel said to the prophet when he came to shew him the pattern of the temple, "Son of man," says he, "behold with thine eyes, and hear with thine ears, and set thine heart upon all that I shall shew thee; for to the intent that I might shew them unto thee art thou brought hither;" Ezek. xl. 4. So to the intent that God might shew to the Publican the evil of his ways, therefore was he brought under the power of convictions, and the terrors of the law; and he also, like a good learner, gave good heed unto that lesson that now he was learning of God; for he would not lift up so much as his eyes to heaven.

Looking downwards doth ofttimes bespeak men very ponderous and deep in their cogitations; also that the matter about which in their minds they are now concerned hath taken great hold of their spirits. The Publican hath now new things, great things, and long-lived things, to concern himself about: his sins, the curse, with death, and hell, began now to stare him in the face: wherefore it was no time now to let his heart, or his eyes, or his cogitations, wander, but to be fixed, and to be vehemently applying of himself (as a sinner) to the God of heaven for mercy.

Few know the weight of sin. When the guilt thereof takes hold of the conscience, it commands homewards all the faculties of the soul. No man can go out or off now: now he is wind-bound, or, as Paul says, "caught:" now he is made to possess bitter days, bitter nights, bitter hours, bitter thoughts; nor can he shift them, for his sin is ever before him. As David said, "For I acknowledge my transgressions: and my sin is ever before me,"--in my eye, and sticketh fast in every one of my thoughts; Psalm li. 3.

"He would not lift up so much as his eyes to heaven, but smote upon his breast." This was the third and last of his gestures; he "Smote upon his breast," to wit, with his hand, or with his fist. I read of several gestures with the hand and foot, according to the working and passions of the mind. It is said, "Balak smote his hands together," being angry because that Balaam had blessed and not cursed for him the children of Israel.

God says also, that he had smitten his hands together at the sins of the children of Israel. God also bids the prophet stamp with his feet, and smite with his hand upon his thigh (Num. xxiv. 10; Ezek. xxii. 13; vi. 11; xxi. 12), upon sundry occasions, and at several enormities; but the Publican here is said to smite upon his breast. And,

1. Smiting upon the breast betokeneth sorrow for something done. This is an experiment common among men; and indeed, therefore (as I take it), doth our Lord Jesus put him under this gesture in the act and exercise of his repentance, because it is that which doth most lively set it forth.

Suppose a man comes to great damage for some folly that he has wrought, and he be made sorrowful for (being and) doing such folly, there is nothing more common than for such a man (if he may) to walk to and fro in the room where he is, with head hung down, fetching ever and anon a bitter sigh, and smiting himself upon the breast in his dejected condition: "But smote upon his breast, saying, God be merciful to me a sinner."

2. Smiting upon the breast is sometimes a token of indignation and abhorrence of something thought upon. I read in Luke, that when Christ was crucified, those spectators that stood to behold the barbarous usage that he endured at the hands of his enemies, smote their breasts and returned. "And all the people (says Luke) that came together to that sight, beholding the things which were done, smote their breasts and returned;" Luke xxiii. 48. Smote their breasts; that is, in token of indignation against, and abhorrence of, the cruelty that was used to the Son of God.

Here also we have our Publican smiting upon his breast in token of indignation against, and abhorrence of, his former life; and indeed, without indignation against, and abhorrence of, his former life, his repentance had not been good. Wherefore the apostle doth make indignation against sin, and against ourselves, one of the signs of true repentance; 2 Cor. vii. 11; and his indignation against sin in general, and against his former life in particular, was manifested by his smiting upon the breast, even as Ephraim's smiting upon the thigh was a sign and token of his: "Surely (says he), after that I was turned, I repented: and after that I was instructed, I smote upon my thigh: I was ashamed, yea, even confounded, because I did bear the reproach of my youth;" Jer. xxxi. 19. Man, when he vehemently dislikes a thing, is very apt to shew a dislike to that thing by this or another outward gesture; as in snuffing or snorting at it, or in deriding; or, as some say, in blowing of their noses at it; Ezek. viii. 17; Mal. i. 13. But the Publican here chooseth rather to use this most solemn posture; for smiting upon the breast seems to imply a more serious, solemn, grave way or manner of dislike, than any of those last mentioned do.

3. Smiting upon the breast seems to intimate a quarrel with the heart, for beguiling, deluding, flattering, seducing, and enticing of him to sin; for as conviction for sin begets in man (I mean if it be thorough) a sense of the sore and plague of the heart, so repentance (if it be right) begets in man an outcry against the heart; forasmuch as by that light, by which repentance takes occasion, the sinner is made to see that the heart is the fountain and well-spring of sin. "For from within, out of the heart of men, proceed evil thoughts, adulteries, covetousness," &c.; Mark vii. 21-23. And hence it is that commonly young converts do complain so of their hearts, calling them wicked, treacherous, deceitful, desperate ones.

Indeed, one difference between true and false repentance lieth in this. The man that truly repents crieth out of his heart; but the other, as Eve, upon the serpent, or something else. And that the Publican perceived his heart to be naught, I conclude, by his smiting upon his breast.

4. Smiting upon the breast seems to intimate one apprehensive of some new, sudden, strange, and amazing thing; as when a man sees some strange sight in the air, or heareth some sudden or dismal sound in the clouds; why, as he is struck into a deep damp in his mind, so it is a wonder if he can keep or hold back from smiting upon his breast.

Now, oftentimes a sight of God and sense of sin comes to the sinner like a flash of lightning (not for short continuance, but) for suddeness, and so for surprisal; so that the sinner is struck, taken and captivated to his own amazement, with what so unexpectedly is come upon him. It is said of Paul at his conversion, that when conviction of his bad life took fast hold of his conscience, he trembled, and was astonished (Acts ix. 6); and although we read not of any particular circumstance of his behaviour under his conviction outwardly, yet it is almost impossible but he must have had some, and those of the most solid sort. For there is such a sympathy betwixt the soul and the body, that the one cannot be in distress or comfort, but the other must partake of and also signify the same. If it be comfort, then it is shewn by leaping, skipping, cheerfulness of the countenance, or some other outward gesture. If it be sorrow or heaviness of spirit, then that is shewed by the body, in weeping, sighing, groaning, shaking of the head, a louring countenance, stamping, smiting upon the thigh or breast, as here the Publican did.

We must not, therefore, look upon these outward actions or gestures of the Publican to be empty, insignificant things; but to be such, that in truth did express and shew the temper, frame, and complexion of his soul. For Christ, the wisdom of God, hath mentioned them to that very end, that in and by them might be held forth, and that men might see as in a glass, the very emblem of a converted and truly penitent sinner. He "smote upon his breast."

5. Smiting upon the breast is sometimes to signify a mixture of distrust, joined with hope. And, indeed, in young converts, hope and distrust, or a degree of despair, do work and answer one another, as doth the noise of the balance of the watch in the pocket. Life and death is always the motion of the mind then, and this noise continues until faith is stronger grown, and until the soul is better acquainted with the methods and ways of God with a sinner. Yea, were but a carnal man in a convert's heart, and could see, he could discern these two, to wit, hope and fear, to have continual motion in the soul; wrestling and opposing one another, as doth light and darkness in striving for the victory.

And hence it is that you find such people so fickle and uncertain in their spirits; now on the mount, then in the valleys; now in the sunshine, then in the shade: now warm, then frozen; now bonny and blithe, then in a moment pensive and sad, as thinking of a portion nowhere but in hell. This will cause smiting on the breast; nor can I imagine that the Publican was as yet farther than thus far in the Christian's progress.

6. Smiting upon the breast seems to intimate, that the party so doing is very apprehensive of some great loss that he has sustained, either by negligence, carelessness, foolishness, or the like. And this is the way in which men do lose their souls. Now, to lose a thing, a great thing, the only choice thing that a man has, negligently, carelessly, foolishly, or the like, why, it puts aggravations into the thoughts of the loss that the man has sustained, and aggravations into the thoughts of them go out of the soul, and come in upon a sudden, even as the bailiff or the king's serjeant-at-arms, and at every appearance of them, makes the soul start; and starting, it smites upon the breast.

I might multiply particulars; but to be brief, we have before us a sensible soul, a sorrowful soul, a penitent soul; one that prays indeed, that prays sensibly, affectionately, effectually; one that sees his loss, that fears and trembles before God in consideration of it, and one that knows no way but the right way, to secure himself from perishing, to wit, by having humble and hearty recourse to the God of heaven for mercy.

I should now come to speak something by way of use and application: but before I do that, I will briefly draw up, and present you with a few conclusions that in my judgment do naturally flow from the text; therefore in this place I will read over the text again.

"Two men went up into the temple to pray; the one a Pharisee, the other a Publican. The Pharisee stood and prayed thus with himself, God, I thank thee, that I am not as other men are, extortioners, unjust, adulterers, or even as this Publican. I fast twice in the week, I give tithes of all that I possess. And the Publican standing afar off would not lift up so much as his eyes unto heaven, but smote upon his breast, saying, God be merciful to me a sinner."

From these words I gather these several conclusions, with these inferences.

1. It doth not always follow, that they that pray do know God, or love him, or trust in him. This conclusion is evident by the Pharisee in the text; he prayed, but he knew not God, he loved not God, he trusted not in God; that is, he knew him not in his Son, nor loved, nor trusted in him. He was, though a praying man, far off from this.

Whence it may be inferred, that those that pray not at all cannot be good, cannot know, love, or trust in God. For if the star, though it shine, is not the sun, then surely a clod of dirt cannot be the sun. Why, a praying man doth as far outstrip a non-praying man as a star outstrips a clod of earth. A non-praying man lives like a beast. "The ox knows his owner, and the ass his master's crib; but this man doth not know, but this man doth not consider;" Isa. i. 3. The prayerless man is therefore of no religion, except he be an Atheist, or an Epicurean. Therefore the non-praying man is numbered among the heathens, and among those that know not God, and is appointed and designed by the sentence of the word to the fearful wrath of God; Psal. lxxix. 6; Jer. x. 25.

2. A second conclusion is, That the man that prays, if in his prayer he pleads for acceptance, either in whole or in part, for his own good deeds, is in a miserable state. This also is gathered from the Pharisee here; he prayed, but in this prayer he pleaded his own good deeds for acceptance, that is, of his person, and therefore

went down to his house unjustified. And he is in this condition that doth thus. The conclusion is true, forasmuch as the Pharisee mentioned in the parable is not so spoken of for the sake of that sect of men, but to caution, forewarn, and bid all men take heed, that they by doing as he, procure not their rejection of God, and be sent away from his presence unjustified. I do therefore infer from hence, that if he that pleadeth his own good doing for personal acceptance with God be thus miserable, then he that teacheth men so to do is much more miserable.

We always conclude, that a ring-leader in an evil way is more blame- worthy than those that are led of him. This falls hard upon the leading Socinians and others, who teach that men's works make their persons accepted of God.

True, they say, through Christ; but that is brought in merely to delude the simple with, and is an horrible lie; for we read not in all the word of God as to personal justification in the sight of God from the curse (and that is the question under consideration), that it must be by man's righteousness as made prevalent by Christ's, but contrariwise, by his and his only, without the deeds, works, or righteousness of the law, which is our righteousness. Wherefore, I say, the teachers and leaders of this doctrine have the greater sin.

3. A third conclusion is, They that use high and flaunting language in prayer, their simplicity and godly sincerity is to be questioned as to the doing of that duty sincerely. This still flows from our text; the Pharisee greatly used this: for higher and more flaunting language can hardly be found than in the Pharisee's mouth; nor will ascribing to God by the same mouth laud and praise help the business at all: for to be sure, where the effect is base and rotten, the cause cannot be good.

The Pharisee would hold himself that he was not as other men, and then gives thanks to God for this: but the conclusion was most vilely false, and therefore the praise for it could not but be foolish, vain, and frivolous. Whence I infer, that if to use such language in prayer is dangerous, then to affect the use thereof is yet more dangerous. Prayer must be made with humble hearts and sensible words, and of that we have treated before; wherefore high, flaunting, swelling words of vanity, become not a sinner's mouth; no, not at any time; much less when he comes to, and presents himself before God in that solemn duty of prayer. But, I say, there are some that so affect the Pharisee's mode, that they cannot be well if in some sort or other they be not in the practice of it, not knowing what they say, nor whereof they affirm; but these are greatly addicted to hypocrisy and desire of vain-glory, especially if the sound of their words be within the reach of other men's ears.

4. A fourth conclusion is, That reformation and amendment, though good, and before men, are nothing as to justification with God. This is manifest by the condition of our Pharisee: he was a reformed man, a man beyond others for personal righteousness, yet he went out of the temple from God unjustified; his works came to nothing with God. Hence I infer, that the man that hath nothing to commend him to God of his own, yet stands as fair before God for justification, and so acceptance, as any other man in the world.

5. A fifth conclusion is, It is the sensible sinner, the self- bemoaning sinner, the self-judging sinner, the self-abhorring sinner, and the self-condemning sinner, whose prayers prevail with God for mercy. Hence I infer, that one reason why men make so many prayers, and prevail no more with God is, because their prayers are rather the floatings of Pharisaical fancies than the fruits of sound sense of sin, and sincere desires of enjoying God in mercy, and in the fruits of the Holy Ghost.

The Codes Of Hammurabi And Moses
W. W. Davies

QTY

The discovery of the Hammurabi Code is one of the greatest achievements of archaeology, and is of paramount interest, not only to the student of the Bible, but also to all those interested in ancient history...

Religion   ISBN: *1-59462-338-4*   **Pages:132**

MSRP $12.95

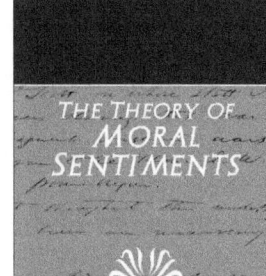

The Theory of Moral Sentiments
Adam Smith

QTY

This work from 1749. contains original theories of conscience amd moral judgment and it is the foundation for systemof morals.

Philosophy ISBN: *1-59462-777-0*   **Pages:536**

MSRP $19.95

Jessica's First Prayer
Hesba Stretton

QTY

In a screened and secluded corner of one of the many railway-bridges which span the streets of London there could be seen a few years ago, from five o'clock every morning until half past eight, a tidily set-out coffee-stall, consisting of a trestle and board, upon which stood two large tin cans, with a small fire of charcoal burning under each so as to keep the coffee boiling during the early hours of the morning when the work-people were thronging into the city on their way to their daily toil...

Pages:84

Childrens   ISBN: *1-59462-373-2*   *MSRP $9.95*

My Life and Work
Henry Ford

QTY

Henry Ford revolutionized the world with his implementation of mass production for the Model T automobile. Gain valuable business insight into his life and work with his own auto-biography... "We have only started on our development of our country we have not as yet, with all our talk of wonderful progress, done more than scratch the surface. The progress has been wonderful enough but..."

Pages:300

Biographies/   ISBN: *1-59462-198-5*   *MSRP $21.95*

The Art of Cross-Examination
Francis Wellman

I presume it is the experience of every author, after his first book is published upon an important subject, to be almost overwhelmed with a wealth of ideas and illustrations which could readily have been included in his book, and which to his own mind, at least, seem to make a second edition inevitable. Such certainly was the case with me; and when the first edition had reached its sixth impression in five months, I rejoiced to learn that it seemed to my publishers that the book had met with a sufficiently favorable reception to justify a second and considerably enlarged edition. ...

Reference   **ISBN: *1-59462-647-2***   **Pages:412**
                                                MSRP $19.95

On the Duty of Civil Disobedience
Henry David Thoreau

Thoreau wrote his famous essay, On the Duty of Civil Disobedience, as a protest against an unjust but popular war and the immoral but popular institution of slave-owning. He did more than write—he declined to pay his taxes, and was hauled off to gaol in consequence. Who can say how much this refusal of his hastened the end of the war and of slavery ?

Law   **ISBN: *1-59462-747-9***   **Pages:48**
                                                MSRP $7.45

Dream Psychology Psychoanalysis for Beginners
Sigmund Freud

Sigmund Freud, born Sigismund Schlomo Freud (May 6, 1856 - September 23, 1939), was a Jewish-Austrian neurologist and psychiatrist who co-founded the psychoanalytic school of psychology. Freud is best known for his theories of the unconscious mind, especially involving the mechanism of repression; his redefinition of sexual desire as mobile and directed towards a wide variety of objects; and his therapeutic techniques, especially his understanding of transference in the therapeutic relationship and the presumed value of dreams as sources of insight into unconscious desires.

Dream Psychology
Psychoanalysis for Beginners

Sigmund Freud

Psychology   **ISBN: *1-59462-905-6***   **Pages:196**
                                                MSRP $15.45

The Miracle of Right Thought
Orison Swett Marden

Believe with all of your heart that you will do what you were made to do. When the mind has once formed the habit of holding cheerful, happy, prosperous pictures, it will not be easy to form the opposite habit. It does not matter how improbable or how far away this realization may see, or how dark the prospects may be, if we visualize them as best we can, as vividly as possible, hold tenaciously to them and vigorously struggle to attain them, they will gradually become actualized, realized in the life. But a desire, a longing without endeavor, a yearning abandoned or held indifferently will vanish without realization.

Pages:360

Self Help   **ISBN: *1-59462-644-8***   *MSRP $25.45*

The Rosicrucian Cosmo-Conception Mystic Christianity *by Max Heindel*   ISBN: *1-59462-188-8*   **$38.95**
The Rosicrucian Cosmo-conception is not dogmatic, neither does it appeal to any other authority than the reason of the student. It is: not controversial, but is: sent forth in the, hope that it may help to clear...   New Age/Religion Pages 646

Abandonment To Divine Providence *by Jean-Pierre de Caussade*   ISBN: *1-59462-228-0*   **$25.95**
"The Rev. Jean Pierre de Caussade was one of the most remarkable spiritual writers of the Society of Jesus in France in the 18th Century. His death took place at Toulouse in 1751. His works have gone through many editions and have been republished...   Inspirational/Religion Pages 400

Mental Chemistry *by Charles Haanel*   ISBN: *1-59462-192-6*   **$23.95**
Mental Chemistry allows the change of material conditions by combining and appropriately utilizing the power of the mind. Much like applied chemistry creates something new and unique out of careful combinations of chemicals the mastery of mental chemistry...   New Age Pages 354

The Letters of Robert Browning and Elizabeth Barret Barrett 1845-1846 vol II   ISBN: *1-59462-193-4*   **$35.95**
by Robert Browning and Elizabeth Barrett   Biographies Pages 596

Gleanings In Genesis (volume I) *by Arthur W. Pink*   ISBN: *1-59462-130-6*   **$27.45**
Appropriately has Genesis been termed "the seed plot of the Bible" for in it we have, in germ form, almost all of the great doctrines which are afterwards fully developed in the books of Scripture which follow...   Religion/Inspirational Pages 420

The Master Key *by L. W. de Laurence*   ISBN: *1-59462-001-6*   **$30.95**
In no branch of human knowledge has there been a more lively increase of the spirit of research during the past few years than in the study of Psychology, Concentration and Mental Discipline. The requests for authentic lessons in Thought Control, Mental Discipline and...   New Age/Business Pages 422

The Lesser Key Of Solomon Goetia *by L. W. de Laurence*   ISBN: *1-59462-092-X*   **$9.95**
This translation of the first book of the "Lernegton" which is now for the first time made accessible to students of Talismanic Magic was done, after careful collation and edition, from numerous Ancient Manuscripts in Hebrew, Latin, and French...   Magic/Occult Pages 92

Rubaiyat Of Omar Khayyam *by Edward Fitzgerald*   ISBN:*1-59462-332-5*   **$13.95**
Edward Fitzgerald, whom the world has already learned, in spite of his own efforts to remain within the shadow of anonymity, to look upon as one of the rarest poets of the century, was born at Bredfield, in Suffolk, on the 31st of March, 1809. He was the third son of John Purcell...   Music Pages 172

Ancient Law *by Henry Maine*   ISBN: *1-59462-128-4*   **$29.95**
The chief object of the following pages is to indicate some of the earliest ideas of mankind, as they are reflected in Ancient Law, and to point out the relation of those ideas to modern thought.   Religiom/History Pages 452

Far-Away Stories *by William J. Locke*   ISBN: *1-59462-129-2*   **$19.45**
"Good wine needs no bush, but a collection of mixed vintages does. And this book is just such a collection. Some of the stories I do not want to remain buried for ever in the museum files of dead magazine-numbers an author's not unpardonable vanity..."   Fiction Pages 272

Life of David Crockett *by David Crockett*   ISBN: *1-59462-250-7*   **$27.45**
"Colonel David Crockett was one of the most remarkable men of the times in which he lived. Born in humble life, but gifted with a strong will, an indomitable courage, and unremitting perseverance...   Biographies/New Age Pages 424

Lip-Reading *by Edward Nitchie*   ISBN: *1-59462-206-X*   **$25.95**
Edward B. Nitchie, founder of the New York School for the Hard of Hearing, now the Nitchie School of Lip-Reading, Inc, wrote "LIP-READING Principles and Practice". The development and perfecting of this meritorious work on lip-reading was an undertaking...   How-to Pages 400

A Handbook of Suggestive Therapeutics, Applied Hypnotism, Psychic Science   ISBN: *1-59462-214-0*   **$24.95**
by Henry Munro   Health/New Age/Health/Self-help Pages 376

A Doll's House: and Two Other Plays *by Henrik Ibsen*   ISBN: *1-59462-112-8*   **$19.95**
Henrik Ibsen created this classic when in revolutionary 1848 Rome. Introducing some striking concepts in playwriting for the realist genre, this play has been studied the world over.   Fiction/Classics/Plays 308

The Light of Asia *by sir Edwin Arnold*   ISBN: *1-59462-204-3*   **$13.95**
In this poetic masterpiece, Edwin Arnold describes the life and teachings of Buddha. The man who was to become known as Buddha to the world was born as Prince Gautama of India but he rejected the worldly riches and abandoned the reigns of power when...   Religion/History/Biographies Pages 170

The Complete Works of Guy de Maupassant *by Guy de Maupassant*   ISBN: *1-59462-157-8*   **$16.95**
"For days and days, nights and nights, I had dreamed of that first kiss which was to consecrate our engagement, and I knew not on what spot I should put my lips..."   Fiction/Classics Pages 240

The Art of Cross-Examination *by Francis L. Wellman*   ISBN: *1-59462-309-0*   **$26.95**
Written by a renowned trial lawyer, Wellman imparts his experience and uses case studies to explain how to use psychology to extract desired information through questioning.   How-to/Science/Reference Pages 408

Answered or Unanswered? *by Louisa Vaughan*   ISBN: *1-59462-248-5*   **$10.95**
Miracles of Faith in China   Religion Pages 112

The Edinburgh Lectures on Mental Science (1909) *by Thomas*   ISBN: *1-59462-008-3*   **$11.95**
This book contains the substance of a course of lectures recently given by the writer in the Queen Street Hail, Edinburgh. Its purpose is to indicate the Natural Principles governing the relation between Mental Action and Material Conditions...   New Age/Psychology Pages 148

Ayesha *by H. Rider Haggard*   ISBN: *1-59462-301-5*   **$24.95**
Verily and indeed it is the unexpected that happens! Probably if there was one person upon the earth from whom the Editor of this, and of a certain previous history, did not expect to hear again...   Classics Pages 380

Ayala's Angel *by Anthony Trollope*   ISBN: *1-59462-352-X*   **$29.95**
The two girls were both pretty, but Lucy who was twenty-one who supposed to be simple and comparatively unattractive, whereas Ayala was credited, as her Bombwhat romantic name might show, with poetic charm and a taste for romance. Ayala when her father died was nineteen...   Fiction Pages 484

The American Commonwealth *by James Bryce*   ISBN: *1-59462-286-8*   **$34.45**
An interpretation of American democratic political theory. It examines political mechanics and society from the perspective of Scotsman James Bryce   Politics Pages 572

Stories of the Pilgrims *by Margaret P. Pumphrey*   ISBN: *1-59462-116-0*   **$17.95**
This book explores pilgrims religious oppression in England as well as their escape to Holland and eventual crossing to America on the Mayflower, and their early days in New England...   History Pages 268

QTY

The Fasting Cure *by Sinclair Upton*   ISBN: *1-59462-222-1*   **$13.95**
In the Cosmopolitan Magazine for May, 1910, and in the Contemporary Review (London) for April, 1910, I published an article dealing with my experiences in fasting. I have written a great many magazine articles, but never one which attracted so much attention... New Age/Self Help/Health Pages 164

Hebrew Astrology *by Sepharial*   ISBN: *1-59462-308-2*   **$13.45**
In these days of advanced thinking it is a matter of common observation that we have left many of the old landmarks behind and that we are now pressing forward to greater heights and to a wider horizon than that which represented the mind-content of our progenitors... Astrology Pages 144

Thought Vibration or The Law of Attraction in the Thought World   ISBN: *1-59462-127-6*   **$12.95**

by William Walker Atkinson   Psychology/Religion Pages 144

Optimism *by Helen Keller*   ISBN: *1-59462-108-X*   **$15.95**
Helen Keller was blind, deaf, and mute since 19 months old, yet famously learned how to overcome these handicaps, communicate with the world, and spread her lectures promoting optimism. An inspiring read for everyone... Biographies/Inspirational Pages 84

Sara Crewe *by Frances Burnett*   ISBN: *1-59462-360-0*   **$9.45**
In the first place, Miss Minchin lived in London. Her home was a large, dull, tall one, in a large, dull square, where all the houses were alike, and all the sparrows were alike, and where all the door-knockers made the same heavy sound... Childrens/Classic Pages 88

The Autobiography of Benjamin Franklin *by Benjamin Franklin*   ISBN: *1-59462-135-7*   **$24.95**
The Autobiography of Benjamin Franklin has probably been more extensively read than any other American historical work, and no other book of its kind has had such ups and downs of fortune. Franklin lived for many years in England, where he was agent... Biographies/History Pages 332

Name	
Email	
Telephone	
Address	
City, State ZIP	

☐ **Credit Card**   ☐ **Check / Money Order**

Credit Card Number	
Expiration Date	
Signature	

Please Mail to: Book Jungle
                    PO Box 2226
                    Champaign, IL 61825
or Fax to: *630-214-0564*

ORDERING INFORMATION

web: *www.bookjungle.com*
email: *sales@bookjungle.com*
fax: *630-214-0564*
mail: *Book Jungle PO Box 2226 Champaign, IL 61825*
or PayPal *to sales@bookjungle.com*

Please contact us for bulk discounts

DIRECT-ORDER TERMS

**20% Discount if You Order
Two or More Books**
Free Domestic Shipping!
Accepted: Master Card, Visa,
Discover, American Express

www.ingramcontent.com/pod-product-compliance
Lightning Source LLC
Chambersburg PA
CBHW080747250626
47162CB00010B/3049